No Evil is Wide

No Evil is Wide

Randall Watson

Lake Dallas, Texas

Printed in the United States of America

FIRST EDITION
Requests for permission to reproduce material from this work should be sent to:

Permissions
Madville Publishing LLC
P.O. Box 358
Lake Dallas, TX 75065

ACKNOWLEDGMENTS
No Evil Is Wide is a revised version of *Petals*, submitted under the heteronym Ellis Reece, which received the 2006/07 Quarterly West prize in the novella category, judged by Brett Lott.

Cover Art by Charles Moody
Author Photograph by Linda Daigle

ISBN: 978-1-948692-06-9 paperback, and 978-1-948692-07-6 ebook
Library of Congress Control Number: 2018948235

"Anyone who cannot come to terms with his life while he is alive needs one hand to ward off a little his despair over his fate—he has little success in this—but with his other hand he can note down what he sees among the ruins, for he sees different (and more) things than do the others; after all, dead as he is in his own life time, he is the real survivor. This assumes that he does not need both hands, or more hands than he has, in his struggle against despair."

—Franz Kafka, *Diaries*, vol. 2 (196) Oct. 19, 1921

Things are not what they appear to be: nor are they otherwise.

—*Surangama Sutra*

The apparition of these faces in the crowd;
Petals on a wet, black bough.

—Ezra Pound

Chapter 1

Red Dogs Under Her Regal Legs

We watched the truck burn. We sat on the roof of a ten story apartment building, the cheap tubular aluminum lawn chairs with the woven nylon seats that were built to fray and bend buckling beneath us, and watched it, the truck, a small blue Toyota, burn. It was, so to speak, how we spent our evenings. It was something we were good at, watching the small fires below grow bright and darken. You could say it was personal, economical— our shared form of transportation.

I'd met her down by Cypress Avenue on one of those streets close to the waterfront, a pile of crumbling drywall and splintered two-by-fours on the corner, the little sheetrock screws scattered rusted on the oil dark-ened ground like the shells of dead insects. She was standing in front of a wall of white-washed brick and had assumed the character of a silhouette, as though she needed all that whiteness behind her to make her visible.

1

It might have been her smallness, but unlike the other girls she was not desirable in the raw way that men who hate themselves are drawn to. With her child's body, small-breasted, thin, what men sought in her, I think, was the contour of an innocence (as if the size of a thing somehow bespoke its morality) they had forgotten the shape of, a kind of vague nostalgia. They were the sort of men who thought that all they wanted was to talk, as if there were something in the exchange that could redeem them, and they were willing to pay for that redemption. But the talk, as she said, always turned dirty, and I knew how it had failed them, how the silence grew large and impatient, an implacable presence only the body could pretend to deny. Touching her, they must have sensed, was a kind of lie, a postponement, a way of dying. And yet there they were, sweating ever so slightly in their leather seats, dimming the headlights, their hands extended, reaching towards her.

There Is No End To It

Do not wonder how I know these things. Know only that I never touched her. I have my own love and it protects me, a nameless figuring, like the blur of lavender on a roadside that keeps a driver alert, or a child on my shoulder, mute and barely visible, who accompanies me everywhere. There is no end to it. Call it a blend of shade and pale transparencies, of memory, white chalk on brownstone facade, the flurry of a flock

2

of sparrows as they descend to the pavement, a woman who exits a parkway. Call it the spark inside these things that knows no obstruction. Call it cipher, cinder, angel, whatever you will. Call it shuffle or asphalt. Bright mirror. Hawaiian shirt.

What I Do

Maybe it was the little metal lunchbox that rested by her feet as she waited for customers, maybe it was the Pixie Stick she held to her lips, tapping the sweet powder onto her tongue as the dark cars cruised by, but I watched for two hours before I decided. I wasn't looking for a child, but what I saw was a woman who looked like one, and finding her there that day was something I did to go on living. It's what I'm paid for.

My job is to find the missing. Not the ones on paper who disappear from courtside after a basketball game at the local high school. Not the ones in the police files. In this line of work there are no anxious parents waiting on the telephone or sitting on park benches staring at their coffee. When a girl rides out on her bicycle into the afternoon and does not return I am not the one they call to search for clues among the gray and white houses, neighborhoods with stylish numbers, frontages of smooth-barked crepe myrtle in profuse white blossom. The distances I seek have addresses. The people I meet have favorite songs and cell phones and listed numbers. Such is the landscape of disappearances, the geography of absence, that the outward shape is sometimes palpable, might have a name, a job in the city, a quiet place to go to when the day has ended, an alarm to wake them when the day begins. They possess, as I sometimes call it, location. There is a way to find them.

First Encounter

I drove an old Chevy Chevette with the hatch taped down and this made me unnoticeable. So when I got out of the car he didn't see me. Maybe if he'd let go of her wrist it all would have been different, but he didn't. It doesn't matter. As one gets older one learns to accept the simple substantiality of events. Or at least to pretend to.

When I approached him he ignored me. "Excuse me, sir," I said, and he looked at me as though I were going to ask him for bus fare or gas money. So I hit him, with a small brass pipe, slightly to the side and just above the left eye, not hard enough to shatter bone but hard enough to draw blood and drop him. I am not a violent man, but when it is called for it should be quick and to the point, what I think of as an efficient kindness, a concise use of language. When he fell I pinned him to the ground with a knee and jerked his head back by the hair, holding his face up to the sky:

"You see the moon, asshole? That moon says go."
And then I left him there, trying to rise.

On Solitude

She was not there when I stepped away from him. She had run away, I suppose, as people do, around a corner, as people say, into a darkness. But I did not go after her. There is a blindness in departures, and its gift is stillness. To follow her would have been futile, a refusal to acknowledge the limitations of force. All true meetings are mutualities. Each of us is our own wilderness and each topography has its own rule, a distance from which, with a little grace, a closeness sometimes emerges, the small breath beneath even the simplest word. My time would come later. All I needed to do was to return.

Chapter 2

Carpenter Wells

He lay there for a moment, waiting. Raised his hand to it, the small ridge of bone above the eye where he had been struck, his blood racing its trail onto his hair and neck, a little pool of it, black like tar, gathered on the street beneath him.

As he sat up the rage grew in him—the image of the girl's face like a small party balloon that swayed gently in and out of his vision, her mouth swollen and disfigured by an invisible internal pressure that seemed to inhabit everything he saw.

I am Carpenter Wells, he thought, And I hate the world—though the thought was not a realization or a phrase or a spoken thing, but a rule that lived unselfconsciously within him, the kind of innate grammar that can govern the years of a man's expression.

Blood, he thought, as he looked at his fingers, tasting them with his lips and mouth—My blood. And he stood there, eyes closed, trying to see the world sideways, again, that he might recall my face and shadow, their suddenness clear and moving at the edge of his world, which was turning.

The One in the Many; The Many in the One

Words are like rain—they fall from the mouth—a history and a simultaneity—worlds hidden within them. But like the rain, the rain that comes from the north or south or east or west, we tend to think of them as possessing a kind of exclusivity, as if the rain itself were something separate from the air, immediate and unencumbered, as though when one said rain one spoke of water only, of water descending, as though there were a solitude to the falling that had not known of wind or ocean or the heat that lies behind the accompanying coolness, the immensity of continents, the height of the air—as if to speak were simple, to tell one's story.

Yet things are never so ready, are never such, or so clear, even if they are willing to be. In each utterance, there is a field of motion, a grief of birth and greeting and timeliness, a love of accidents and shouting, of meeting and departure. Not a stillness of meaning, but its illusion—where the dragonfly, like the hummingbird, pauses, the wind, like the mother or father passing the doorway of a sleeping child, pauses, the sun, like a blossom of smoke and drifting, pauses, and then passes on.

We call it history.

And so I imagine her, in this moment of quiet, the

many and the one and the one and the many, I watch her move, yes, immediate, palpable, mythic, out into the rain, into the falling water, which is a form of praise for her, a softness that is welcome, a way of speaking. It is why I can see her lifting her hands, touching her face, perhaps, or smoothing her hair as if she were taking a shower and ready to lean forward into the rinse of water. These are the blossomings of an unimaginable force: a face that is wet with its eyes closed, a body that is thin and tense and cold and hard in its pleasure, a voice that is laughing. In this, there is the love of passage, the joy of the divided, sibling lights of morning and evening among the narrow avenues. Here, her need is my salvation—like a kind of love—a need that finds me and that gives, the wordless thing that keeps me, that breath, that enunciation. Our gift.

And thus, I wait. I sit at the diner and wait and eat and wait and watch the new spoons grow gradually dull, their basins freshly cluttered with tiny scratches. I watch the small cars open and close, the big cars, the sidewalk with its blackened foyers, the light above the door across the way wavering like a sixth martini. I watch it all go loud and I watch it all go quiet, the last angry shout of the night made indistinguishable from the first cry of the morning. I wait for her, to see her, to make a way for her, an asking. It is what I'm paid for: it is how I live. Holding my hand out to measure my tiredness: holding my hand out to measure yours.

Her House, Her Home

Her mother was a dark slenderness that seemed to turn away from itself, as if everything she said were a parenthetical statement, as if even the things most dear to her possessed no more than the most tangential significance. I couldn't imagine what kind of parent she had been, what to live with her, coming home from school on long afternoons, would have been like. But there was something almost sacramental about her, and this, I believe, rooted in the forlorn quality of her face and habit, is what made her dear to me: she was one of those people who conveyed the sense that no benefit could come from knowing them, and that to help her might save a part of you you had forgotten, something small and essential in your blood.

The photograph she held out had been taken in a booth at one of those diners that serve meatloaf and macaroni casserole with milkshakes and Cherry Colas. It was old and fading, torn and curling at the edges, but she held it as though she had suddenly realized that she was thirsty and cupped some water in her hand.

The phone number and address, she said, like a confession or a plea, are on the back.

And then, before me, was the face of the woman I would look for: her youth as archetypal as migration or retreat, a girl who was lovely and small, yet with a strained and vacant look, as though something had come between her and the camera, something painful or dangerous, an idea of something, perhaps, or a memory. I looked at her there, and tried to imagine her—a girl you might ask to dance who would smile and say yes and then forget you for months, watching you later, after a basketball game or a pool tournament, with a strained, uncomprehending curiosity, as you, sad, nervously, struggled to pronounce her name.

Figures of Speech

These are the absences: the doll's head the daughter of a famous singer keeps in her purse, and the song that was its body. The one white shoe you saw on the spur road where it passes beneath the parkway. The drunk who flatters his neighbor. Sometimes I think I can hear the voice of something else: the spark that moves through this careful flesh that has forgotten its return. The sparrow's tail as it gathers light.

The Way of the Bodhisattva

There is consequence in a man's genes, a part of his inheritance, his blood, the flavor of his day. It is the face of an inscrutable genesis. A culmination. Karma or Fate. One might say the trees are filled with it: not the approach of spring or winter, or the wind that has recently crossed over water, but the algebraic light with its unknown variables, the habits of shadow the birds emerge from. Here, everything is indirection: what one wants to give is pure metonymy—not the thing itself, but its hopeful idea, its feeling and referent: the red heart of the phallic anthurium, the word at the start of an unending sentence, the chocolate biscotti.

Thus—How can I say it? There is a woman and she is dreaming, someplace, of biochemistry and construction paper, of a river south of Cincinnati, of binder clips and blue juncos, of heat and midnight and the small white pills she believes might brighten it, of lakefront houses and wicker furniture. These are the forms her longing takes: not the sound of the flute but the breath as it seeks the shape of music. Not the illness, but the fever when it rises or breaks. Not the woman sitting with her hands folded, but the reason she unclasps them. These are the gaps in the syntax, the transformations, the proofs of her resilience and her grief and gladness, of her unfinished being. These are the shoutings. These are the dogs with violet tongues. These are the blue lights and the red lights and the green lights her neighbor swore were circling above her the week her father died.

What I am trying to say is there is no end to any of this: the box filled with cancelled checks you keep beneath your bed. The whiteness of the wool that is dipped into the boiling saffron. The silver harmonica. Imagine it—you are like the breath—residual and intricate and burgeoning: something soft and wooden to pass through, a precious metal to frame your passage.

Let us give thanks for it—that our source is musical—our love, a sound—as old as night or rain as they settle onto the hills of earth—a song—and in the notes our fearlessness and our joy.

Chapter 3

New Year Zero: Saint Death

That was the year that people came to believe the world was changed. No one knew how or why, but it was a feeling that spread from one person to the next, from house to house and family to family. Some people called it Fire Monkey, some people called it Ash. Others waved their arms about as though they were telling the sky to stop or they were warning something no one could see that was passing over them. Things seemed to reveal themselves with a new directness, and what we saw was what we had refused, what we saw was the suddenness of things, and how this suddenness could penetrate, like a knife or a splinter of wood, leaving us wavering and dumb and calling.

And so, things, at times, almost imperceptibly, changed, but changed nonetheless. One man raced across the street while crouching. A woman sat on a folding metal chair, bookended by red curtains, taking off her lingerie for a selection of the city leaders. The lies that once soothed us now gave no more than a savage comfort, and what rose inside us was a strained and unsaid thing, a terror, of sorts, not a new knowing but a return, an old color, ancient and almost forgotten. Each object was a signature, a symbol, a sign of the dying that is our deepening: as when a widow listens, for the first time, to her dead husband's favorite symphony, the worlds that turn within her set to and broken by the measure of the strings. Or when one finds, months after the funeral, a note from a friend, generously welcoming you home from your trip to the Antilles. Call it what you will: the Drawer, the Great Idea, the Pocket Dance, for there is a madness in it, a flame that continues. Horrible. The Year of the Snake, of the Turning Eastward, of Granite and Water, of the Burning Hand, the Bright Slipper. It is generic, multiform, nameless, the color of hair amidst the performances of evening, the shape of a twisted foot, of the hand dissociate, dance of the day-garment and the show, of the lovely, large-breasted executive assistant with the tanned investment banker.

Who knows what our lives have become, is not a question. It is our hope, it is what we have been seeking. Not what they have been, but what they are. Think of it like this: it was the week when she returned, the hour that followed the month of waiting, the moment in the half-light and the cold. Meeting her, I recognized, one meets oneself in darkness and amber, a soft glow the color of a tanning bed that has somehow made its way into the air. Do you understand? Can you hear me?

The Meeting

I spoke to her this time. Walked up to her slowly, said my piece about climate, how it becomes, almost unnoticeably, a part of us: the humidity like an assault upon the flesh, the wet air against you, drawing you, like the paper cover of a book, away from yourself. Well, she said, and she looked at me, careful, wary, waiting to see what I might say to her next, what I might do or want, and if she could bear it.

500, I said, I'll give you 500 bucks if you meet me for coffee.

Chapter 4

The First Dream

I am not awake, and yet it is 7:25 and there are church bells ringing—and the roosters have been crowing all night long—at every passing headlight, perhaps, twin suns ascending the little hill that rises from one park to another, and for some reason I think that they are like dogs, though I do not know why, and that someone should shoot them for walking sideways, for that pride that calls out even at darkness when it is first-morning that is theirs—not this blackness that is my sleep and dreaming.

Such are the visions that come to me—the sign of her that is always somehow changing. Now it is a woman's black hair and eyes, like a flood that has made a new river behind the houses of strangers, something that rushes swift and quiet and dangerous through the night like an approaching swarm of ants or beetles, something that glitters, occasionally, in the light of the thin moon— perpetually moving and yet still and unchanging.

These are the visions of her—curious and contradictory: a glance from the passenger seat of a small white car as she passes by. Her face in the open door of a small theatrical library—and her thinness too—her brown slenderness framed by long white translucent curtains all made bright by the outside light that burns above her.

All day I walk—and I see her everywhere: rearranging stuffed giraffes in storefront windows, gazing aimlessly at a display of eyeglasses, hurrying across the street in front of a fast taxi. She giggles beneath her paper mask at the pastry shop. She stops me on the street to sell me jewelry, her eyes as black as the doors of an iron stove, imperturbable, yet glowing faint with light and heat.

These are the days of her comings and goings—days of translucence and twilight, the always changing shape of her eyes and body, mouth of the high plains and mouth of the sea, her breath a wave of the morning, or the breeze that accompanies the first appearance of the sun at the top of the mountain.

Arrivals (I)

When she comes, she comes slow, uncertain, making her way through the little crowd outside, through the cold, through the steam that rises from the breath. But with me, when she sits at my table, unraveling the red scarf from her throat, she is quick, almost harsh. "Coffee," she says, and then she waits for me to speak, for the waiter to come and take her order, for the money that sits in my pocket, that I put gently on the table in front of her, five fresh bills on a paper tablecloth.

"Yes," she says, and reaches her gloved hand out to take it.

How much smaller she is than I remember, her hair cut short like a leather helmet, blue-eyed, pale, lips glittering with the kind of gold men have sought for ages, kneeling at the edge of mud and water.

Her world, I think, is not her own, but a place of refuge. There, beyond the glass and the little tables, is the place that makes her thin and small, that habit of silk and hands, of pockets and creases, dance music slow and distant on the car radio. Prostitute—Addict—Celebrity—Whore. These are our names for it— our metaphors for the new millennium. Passage and barter and flight, our weakness and our thirst, the jealous pleasure of the body that we carry with us, that we keep and store yet runs through our fingers, clear as water. Wealth, we call it. Riches.

What is it that is in her, I think, that builds upon itself, like a shell or a bit of hollow stone that shines when broken, a pair of old boots on the floor under the table with the bowl of wooden fruit on it, this past that is hers, unbidden yet chosen, something she races toward and from, and the injury of that hurry that names her.

She sits there, quiet. Looks at me. "What do you want, " she says, sipping her coffee, pale fingers against the blue mug. "I want to help you," I say, and she pauses, looks away, then turns back to me and spits, slowly, letting it gather on her lips like a leaky pipe or faucet, till it falls, dense, suddenly, and heavy and quick, onto the table.

Arrivals (II)

We make our arrangements. Meet—an extension, of sorts—a retreat or threat—and waver, sometimes, like the flame of a candle, our hearts as dark and unmoving as the wick. There is always, it seems, a nervousness in our approach—a coersion of eyes and angles, face turned toward a window, one hand clutching the thumb of another beneath the table—as though we were like dogs in a cage with the door open—birds with the voices of polished metal.

It seemed to me she hardly knew how to smile—or to look, casually, calmly, into the face of either man or woman without wanting something there, or expecting to find it closed, in its way, filled by its own wanting, its impassiveness barely hidden by the harsh shape of the mouth, a place where there was no room for meeting, no open ground for encounter.

I knew it was the money she agreed to—the hard cash, dense and weighted—not me, my face or manner. It was this she granted, this she trusted, thinking, perhaps mistakenly, she knew its habit and its strength, even its weakness, its anger and its sleep—how it lightens the body when the body moves, or is a sanctuary, a room with a soft couch to sit on when the time for sitting comes: nights when the cars stop a block away, watching, and the sense of emptiness, of the uninhabitable world, begins to spread like a drop of blood in a bowl of water.

"Two weeks," she said. "Here. If you're still alive." And she smiled as if for the first time—like something shiny under a child's bed, something you must want enough to reach for. Not a threat, but a challenge. An invitation.

The Idea of the Good

The Good, you think. The shape of belief, abstraction of the world, yet manifest—palpable and recurrent, flesh and symbol, blood and word and light—their common body.

Like a couple of kids playing outside a little Franciscan chapel above the salt-pots outside Cuzco, terraced pools of water drying crystal white and gathered by young girls whose fingers burn with it.

Was that the Good? Where the sun was hot as the air was thin and the kids filled the buckets first, then the packs they balanced onto the back of a goat and a burro.

Was this their sacred formula—their labor and their burden and their sacrifice—and with them, a blindness—and in that blindness an idea of ourselves, a kind of largeness, inherited or self-imagined—an uncertain grasping, a presumption— a man examining the throat of a cat at the turn of the old millennium, his monocle held, for a moment, in the bright air and light that is near his face but not upon it, telling the gathering crowd about the breath and speech and poetry, how they are graceful and feline and the good and careful man can make a world out of them, an inner world of care and brightness?

Saint Death and the Sacred Circle

Yes. There were mounds of it—the salt—wet and white and burning. And the children, soon joined by others, the light gathering, entered the chapel.

And so I imagined them, not much different than myself, than you, in form only—how we meet and touch—out of our longing—-a small circle in the heart that can find neither wholeness nor exit—our bodies bent down at altars in the dark of the early morning, the heat of the evening, offering up ourselves in whispers that lead us slowly, we believe and hope, towards the light that welcomes us when we re-enter the world.

All this because of the shadow of death—there, in the face of the body, the crude, uninhabited flesh, the unrecognizable face of a loved one. Because of this strangeness—this dull landscape—the sudden green luminescence of a bush or tree enlightened by the rain. A house of sand and dirt. At the end of a cul-de-sac beside the bay that is south and great and unpatrolled, a young boy and girl in their first awakening and disappearance—their fear dispelled by their desire.

My father called it communion: or rather, that what we remember, vaguely, is its remnant, this fragment that is recollection and transport—a kind of faith, but known and remembered, a weight and a balance and an agreement, a membership—a disappearance and a freedom—and a willingness—like the man who is glad to eat his last bit of bread even though it has been blackened, somewhat, who can tell how much, by the fire?

One Form of Hope

She has a name—not an inheritance, but a name—a chosen thing, a kind of understanding, like something you keep safe beneath your coat or shirt, or that emerges, gradually, from the careful channels that are obscured by the flesh yet reign upon it. A discovery and reason.

I will recognize the name. I know this. I will know what it means and where it comes from—how it becomes her—and how it is part of the work—this knowledge that I have—that I take into the places where I live and wander, the young and old men equally insensible by noon, the women as pale as an unwashed cueball—that color of illegal bone or ivory that is the color of resignation and the cruel, forgetful art we know as retreat and mistake for comfort and wealth—our leisure time—our play—our calling.

Sympathy for the Devil

I like the fat ones best, she said. They give you the money and then they just sit there, as though they weren't sure what they had paid for, and all you have to do is act as if you are about to cry, but trying not to, digging through your purse while blinking rapidly, turning your head, for a moment, away from him, your fingers cupping your near eye as though to protect it from some unnoticeable sliver of light that threatens to blind you.

What, they say, and they rest a hand on your shoulder, and you tell them you are hungry and lonely and so far from home or love or salvation you don't know what to do, and when you start to cry they offer comfort and give you money, more money, because they are happy, she said, though she didn't quite see that what they paid for was the chance to believe in something—her, them—and that it is this kind of happiness that people will pay twice for.

Chapter 5

The Commentary

She was cheap, they said. The other girls. New, but cheap. And when a girl is cheap, they said, and new. A stick, they said. As dry as old lipstick or paper, ready to melt or burn. You'll see—one bright flash on a Thursday night and then—nothing but ash—a dark and oily spot on the corner, a day of rain. Shit, they said. And they held their hands out—hands that had learned how to please a man or rob him, girl's hands and women's, open, for a moment only, in the cold air.

Chapter 6

Origins; A Bildungsroman

Story goes my mother left me when I was 5 but I don't remember. Story goes she dropped me off at the Jameson's, the family I stayed with after school, a small family, though Mrs. Jameson was large and liked to laugh a lot and hit her children when she was angry or frightened, which happened frequently. She had named all her children after wine bottles—Amber, Corky, Violet—and she made them clean house and keep silent, though she also made sure the refrigerator was full of their favorite ice creams, the cupboard stocked with their favorite candies. If my memory were better, I'd swear she lived on nothing but sugar and the occasional bit of French bread she cut into thin strips to snack on when she drank, which was every week, Wednesday through Sunday, as regular as the television that kept her company. Who knows why she let me stay—but I was there more than two months before my father came to get me.

Father, I said, when they brought me to him, standing there with his hat in his hand as though he were pretending to be one of those humble Mexican peasants in the movies from the 30s who shows up at the greedy ranchero's hacienda to beg for his beautiful daughter's return.

Father, I said, and he looked at me.

Get in the car.

Chapter 7

Apocalypse of Memory: The Babysitter's House of Adult Intentions

The light was different—it was one of the ways the world had shifted—the light in the air, in the people's eyes, the small light in the refrigerator or the stove, office lights and houses, the moon in its brightness and retreat. This was what the people saw and believed, believed and saw—the shadows becoming, somehow, more informed, capacious, resistant even at midday—like the pale, dark spot on the retina of a man who has glanced too directly at the sun and is temporarily stunned by it— the point of light that is not light yet lingers in his eyes and enters his thoughts and stays with him, sometimes, for hours, an emptiness at the center of his vision.

If absence had a name, the house would have spoken it. Had it been a man, it would have undressed itself. Had it been a woman, it would have cleaned its fingernails with a toothpick, wiping the dark sludge off the wooden tip onto the arm of the couch, which was curved the way the moon is curved when it is a bowl that has been emptied.

Everything about it seemed uncertain and strained. It smelled, almost constantly like hair remover and wet paper towels, or like certain weeds, unnameable, that stain your hands when you pull them from the ground, a smell of onions, warmed and softened by a desk lamp, repulsive, and yet familiar, even strangely attractive, like a ham sandwich that has languished on the counter for over a day, the crust almost crisp and mysteriously darkened.

Everything confused me. Violet appeared each afternoon with a new, shiny, silver balloon clipped to the hem of her skirt, lifting it ever so slightly, enough that I could see her underwear when she sat down or bent over to examine some indecipherable speck on the sidewalk or the stoop. Amber spent days imitating the sounds of appliances—the song of the washing machine and the dryer, roaring sometimes like a blender or a vacuum cleaner, reproducing perfectly the musical elements of the coffee machine or the wet hum of the dishwasher as it rested between cycles.

At night I dreamed—dreams that possessed a dangerous coherence—dreams I could hardly tell from waking.

This was fear. Its uncanny arrival, the body transformed into a threat, a wheel of heat and fire turning inside it. Here were people making coffee, buying salt and flowers, cakes for children who grew large and sleepy in their little rooms. Here were people shopping for oil and instant soup, keys protruding from their fists, wearing their shoes into the sea.

Soon, of course, there were explosions. Buildings trembled. A woman cleaning her car at a gas station was shot in the back of the head by the son of a neighbor who kept his gun hidden in a box of Lucky Charms for years.

This much was clear. What once was distant was now near and made real by its closeness. What once was another's was our own, and feeding, mounting the stairs at the mall, stepping up in its long coat onto the train platform, lighting an extraordinarily large cigar outside the treatment center. Who knew how long it had been there, waiting, latent, an enzyme in the blood, a blank spot on the scantron, a habit of empire. But now it was here—arising—inchoate, mutable, transparent—there in the stained teeth of the lottery winner, the red-hard jacket and skirt of the state representative, in the mouth and its promises, the stiff nipples of the mannequin at the silk boutique by the coffee shop. Isn't it strange how it loves the mask of the ordinary—the gentle buttons on a girl's sweater; the bubbles that cluster at the edge of a bowl of fresh poured milk.

The Social Contract

It is all over the television—on every channel—a rob-
bery gone wrong at a small grocery at the edge of the
city. Inside, three boys, 16, 14, who can know, two with
guns, one with nothing but fear and air and a hunger he
satisfies by gorging himself on peanuts and chocolate
and chips that burn the tongue.

This the cameras tell us: we can see him eating,
stalking the aisles, lifting first a carton of orange juice
to his lips, then a can of soda, his friends, blanketed by
hostages whose faces betray that blend of disbelief and
terror that is nothing but an almost immobile dullness—
his friends peering through the plate glass window and
waving their guns, making their list of demands: forgetfulness, a palace of gold in the mountains, three women
who can sing, as lovely as the moon and as soft as a
feather.

Like the people watching, the reporter, urgent,
almost hysterical, does not seem to know the difference between the rare and the extraordinary—perhaps
because he cannot bear to live in a world in which such
things are common. And who can blame him? And yet
there are those who are denied such comforts, for whatever reasons, who move and act with the knowledge
that our lives are continuously phrased in the distance
that separates one moment from the next, one act or
word from another, until it, whatever it might be, arrives

with an intractable violence—this leap that is the soul of tragedy or grace.

Soon the shots will ring out, the boys lie dead amongst the scattered bags of lentils and pasta, a woman crying, shoulders cradled by the raised arms of a paramedic, her face covered with blood, her left arm gesturing, almost aimlessly, behind her.

Origins II: A Kuntslerroman

All I remember is that Mrs. Jameson called me into the living room—my days there unremarked except by wariness, a pervasive sense of potential terror—to rub her feet, which were large and the pale white color and texture of a tampon wrapper. She had propped them up on the coffee table—angling them away from the television so as not to interfere with her view—and there were small circles of what looked like paint, turquoise and purple, on their bottoms, and a blob that had the texture of cookie dough and the look of a nylon stocking. When I touched them they were damp, and when I rubbed and squeezed, as she commanded, they seemed to put off water or oil, like a bit of fried bread or a sponge, and the more I worked them the more the grease dripped down her feet to form a puddle on the top of the table she rested them upon, stripping the finish and robbing the wood of its stain and color.

Here they are. The faces and their expressions and where they linger. Today it's the fetus in the toilet at the local high school, girls and boys with their mouths open for the camera. Tomorrow it's a mother who drives her two children into the river because only the water can save them, the reporter telling us carefully how the woman strapped the small bodies into the little car seats made and marketed to keep them from harm.

One day we say mother, and we think it is a holy thing, this motherhood, intrinsic, good, burdened by the labor that is its love, bent by it, but never broken. One day we say mother and we mean that each eye is bright and wet and knows its purpose: the roundness of the breast that suckles the hungry, that takes the hunger that is rough and softens it, pliable, giving to it a fullness and a heart, though it is a fullness that gradually trembles and falls and becomes our hunger once again.

You want to see my pet worm, Corky said, backing furtively into the laundry room by the porch where he opened his mouth wide and reached far back into his throat to tug at something, then saying from beneath his tongue—Look, Can you see it?—holding his lips apart as I peered in to see, for a brief, unbelievable second only, something white and glistening retreating back into his throat, disappearing into the darkness there, where it lay hidden, as far as I knew, and hungry, I presumed, hungry enough to leave the body at night to wander the house, entering the noses of the unsuspecting, sleeping household, laying multitudes of small bubbling eggs that would hatch inside you and consume you by morning. Needless to say, I tried desperately to stay awake, and when I woke up, terrified, the first thing I would do each morning was to inspect myself for any sign of violation or entrance—a faint white ring at the edge of a nostril, a shiny crease upon the lip, froth within the ears, a tingling deep inside my belly that seemed to slowly uncoil itself whenever I thought of eating.

Chapter 8

Poor Richard's Almanac

Richard was common. If you had dope he would love you. If you had more dope he would love you more.

The last woman he lived with was slow and fat, but she was rich and Richard gave her all the anger that his body could give, his body hard with it and her body wanting that hardness—wanting her hair pulled back as he entered her from behind—forgetting everyone she'd ever been except for who she became when he was showing her who she could be. For seven months this somehow kept them happy—if you could call it happiness—making their daily trips to the ATM and then the dope house on 14th Street where the cans of peas and corn were thick with dust and they slid their cash through the slick, curved slot at the base of the bullet-proof ticketwindow and whispered through the hole that was cut there for the face and the voice only: this, or that, or another, or more, or help me, please, taking in return the little packets of folded waxed-paper envelopes with the names of weapons written on them—M-16, Silver Bullet, Machete, Iraq.

Who knows why she left him. The waitress at the RedBar says she found a more refined and talkative Ukrainian with a bigger cock, but she is a bitter woman. Normally I wouldn't care, though I know this condemns me, but just yesterday I saw him talking to her, walking her into one of those unlicensed bodegas where they keep the beer in large metal tubs of ice and you drink your wine from plastic glasses the color of blindness, the Puerto Rican girls inside with their hair in curlers, blow jobs in the back for a twenty. Thick Mexican heroin like mud or clay you've got to melt in water to boot up, kicking yourself, as they say, with a dull needle.

Poor Richard. I knew he could not help himself—that what he did he did because it was what made him and was made by him, this thing that gave him a distance from the part of himself he had no name for, that strange calling that was what he followed and took—from himself, from others.

His best found its expression and its proof in what he did and that alone. Everything else was a wish and a comfort. In the act completed was the shadow of an absolute that lived within his character and defined his every impulse—and the distinction made to claim his goodness as his own and yet credit his greed or lust or savagery to some other invasive spirit that surprised and denied him whenever it appeared, was a sham. Whatever his essence, it was like a buried mirror, and he had become a wreckage of habit and reflex, a mouth and a voice, a shape of hunger and its fear.

A Mr. Wells in the making.

Our Father Who Art

We had been driving a long time, the rain now falling, the night with it. It had been day when we started—clear, easy—when my father woke me from my sleep, telling me to get up, dress myself, bring a banana or an orange.

Houses went by—yellow brick the color of sand or depression—lots and fields, and then farmhouses, pastures open and in flower with a few stray horses, the sun hot on the side of my face, the world sleepy and distant. Then fields again. Fence posts leaning, lots with their piles of wire and cement, streets that stunk of rotting peppers. Wooden houses the color and quality of mist and illness, steps without backing, a couple of kids playing with steak knives.

My father pulled the car over and sat there, the darkness growing. The kids looked at us and moved away. The house in front of us was like any other house on the block, small and ruined, but the front door was covered in tattered red foil and had a fraying hedge-green ribbon dangling from its center. Soon a woman with a bag of groceries that sang like wind chimes mounted the steps, struggled with the lock and started cursing, loudly and without restraint, until the door finally opened and she entered the house, leaving nothing to see but what was there already before she had come or gone, the red door shining a bit, the street wet and empty. I don't know how long we sat there, for I soon grew tired and fell asleep, face cold against the glass,

but when I woke we were parked at a diner and my
father sat there counting his money in its brightness—
large coins and small ones, a few tired dollars.

The Mouth of Heaven

Here, there is no fixed number, no certainty, no known
means of arrival or entrance. Everything is mutable, a
dream of correspondences, the illusory edge of the world.

Yet sometimes, like a lover, you can forget yourself
to find it, the flower that blossoms in the gap between
each breath or beat of the blood, your eyelids not even
fluttering, the brightness trembling like wet ice cast
onto a hot sidewalk, the small pools of water spreading.
Sometimes, you can lower yourself too— descend, like
a dissolving lozenge, into the throat, like a thought passing through the quiet castle of the skull, night all silent
and empty—a little motel in the country where the pool
fills with leaves and mildew.

Whatever, there is neither good luck nor bad, no
chip of stone or silver, no eye or knuckle, no sacred
horn—nothing to announce the sudden appearance of
the vehicle but the thing itself: the plum tree on the hill,
the pruning shears, open and on the ground beneath the
man who cleans his gutters.

This is the world, the way to heaven—leaves trembling
in the hedge as the sky darkens, a woman touching the
skin of a man, the night built of a comfort that is speech
enough for her, the sad voice of the morning returning.

Some say it is like love, or the lack of it. That it is one of the names we have for the distances between us, how they become, at times, almost indiscernible, full, at others, empty, like the meaning of a language you can neither speak nor understand, your knowledge as sound and rhythm only.

Heaven, they say, lives in what you choose—the seat you find that is yours to sit in, the shoes that fit and last and make your moving easy—the mind you bring to put inside the things you meet so you might know them as yourself and forgive them. This is heaven: your freedom and your love—how the mind forgets itself to find an illimitable light inside it.

The Plot Thickens

I follow nothing—the unnamed shaking—immeasurable hope.

Turns out Carpenter Wells is loud and angry and has the money to turn his anger into a question, where my blood is its answer.

Find me, then, I say to him, his hired man, his punk, driving around the city in a pair of golf shoes and a portable drill, its half-inch-bit glistening dully on the seat beside him.

Find me.

Breathe on me.

I will show you the light.

Chapter 9

The Name of the Goddess

I cannot tell you her name, though I should like to. Not because I want it only for myself, or that you shouldn't know it, but so you might discover it for yourself, one of the names of love, within you or near you, familiar and wanting. Perhaps it is the name of a girl, afraid of beetles yet sickened by the sound that is made when you crush them beneath your feet, scooping the shattered bodies up with a paper towel. Or maybe it is the name of your girlfriend or wife—the one you met at a place of worship—the color of the sky suggested by evening—a woman who has renounced something to love you and now grows quiet, holding her newborn in her arms and looking out the kitchen window at the apple trees that are in full blossom, the white halos rustling in the wind, the small petals falling, occasionally, in a brief flurry, like errant snowflakes that are the first or last of the year, a verge of purity that settles on the face of the earth and is a premonition of either winter or spring.

This time, however, she was not alone. She came with him—Richard—they came together—sat down—looked at me—his eyes as dark as the bruised skin of an old banana, his arms as skinny as the stem of an apple, no fruit attached.

I, of course, said nothing. Lifted my spoon to stir my coffee, slowly, ever so slowly, then slightly faster, with just enough force to suggest a whirlpool at the heart of it, and the shadow that surfaces, suddenly, then disappears once you have stopped the stirring and removed the spoon—human, almost, in its symbolism, the sea returned to its undinal calm, the face discovering its original contentment, its original peace.

So, she said, You have survived? and she looked at me, curious, hopeful, wanting to give almost half of a thin smile to her mouth, but holding it and waiting, watching me. So I put the five hundred on the table, spreading the bills out like a hand of cards, keeping my eyes on her, careful eyes, open, yet saying nothing. For a moment we sat there, suspended, looking at each other, her with her questions and her doubt, me alone with my knowledge and intentions. But when he started to reach for the money I brought my hand down on it.

This is your money, I said to her. But this time, and I smiled, you have to remove your gloves to take it.

I can tell you her hands were beautiful. Clean. The nails as perfect as small planets, the edge of the moon above the horizon. No scratches or cuts. A cool sheet in summer. Skin as soft as a lamb's ear, or mullein, tiny hairs that dangled like eyelashes on the underside of a leaf.

I thought, then, that she loved them. And I hoped that she would watch them change with age, holding them out in front of herself to marvel at their changes and love them still. I hoped that her hands contained her future, that this brightness was how they spoke, and what they spoke of—a language that was their condition and their shape, a tenderness they would practice and rehearse until it was as natural to her as a breath.

Chapter 10

Gossip and Dying

Some people said it was the rich who had started the bombing. Some people said it was the poor. Others said it was students from the university, or the dropouts who lived under the eaves of the old bridge east of the river, bored and angry and convinced of their purity and ideological clarity. One old woman said it was a bunch of old men who wanted to make something of their lives before they died. The city treasurer said it was a coalition of eco-terrorists who dreamed of groaning at the edge of a fire while they waited for their burritos to warm up in the microwave. Union members insisted it was a group of intellectuals with swollen tongues who lived beneath the city with a drunken revelry of beautiful women who could not admit they liked attention, and a drunken imminence of ugly men who did. Some even dared propose it was the government, or one of the many parties, most of which thrived on fear and the people's need for security—a people who were willing to exchange their freedom for pleasure, a people seduced by a language created to convince them of their own unacknowledged eminence.

Regardless, the bombs went off, a multitude of explosions, yet somehow a singular event which perpetuated itself in the mind of the city, grew large and expansive, a blinding flash at the bank on the corner, a fruit stall erupting into flame.

These are the bodies of the dead—a basket of wood beside the fireplace. A stack of papers, inert now, unmoving. These were the lives—a blankness now upon those interior mysteries that extended themselves throughout the blood, the strained yet graceful volatility of the hands and feet, the mouths that were once wet and shiny.

I call this the burning inside us. Its gradual encroachment, like the curled and browning edge of a white lily desperate for water.

A mother, here. A father. A child. A woman with no family.

Help us.

Getting To Know Her

I can play house, she said, patty cake, do or don't, the recorder. Stationary.

Utensil. Pen. A glass of water, a cup with a crack in it, or a stain, an unclean thing that needs washing, a girl in a burgundy dress with her arms crossed. Ardent revolutionary. Dishwasher, harpist, aspiring singer. The daughter of someone you hate. The girl who walks slowly down the street because she wants you to see her, or the girl who walks slowly because she has nowhere to go and no desire to get there. What do *you* want, she said, making the you of it hard and pointed, as though it might actually include me. A girl with holes in her socks, like a placemat or a doily, her skirt the color of a clean dish, skin as golden as a doughnut or a key, a color for your mouth and hands, body as smooth as a water ride at the county fair, small boat and wet circle, her headband like a thin halo that keeps her hair from her eyes so that you might look away when she turns them toward you.

Some of What I Said To Her: The Inheritance

I am wealthy, you know. Fabulously. Gloriously. Seven days after I turned eighteen my father won 108 million dollars in the lottery, and one morning nine days later— after a week of too many women and too little sleep, his head, slowly, somberly, came to rest upon the kitchen table and stayed there—which was how I found him— face turned toward the side, cheeks and forehead and nose the color of milk, his temple resting next to a bowl of red and yellow cherries, browning, ever so slightly, where the fruit meets the stem.

Father, I used to say—for a year, for two, for twenty—and then I would sit there, incomprehensibly mute, the thing I wished for hidden within a kind of vague immensity that included everything and nothing and could not be spoken, could hardly be noted, except as smoke, for example, when it moves almost invisibly from the lungs through the shadow of a house and into the single panel of light that has entered there, becoming a brilliance of circles and swirls and heavings, the breath made into a facet of vision—a revelation that moves beyond the body, alive, continuous and evolving, both one with the light and air and linked to its origin within us.

It took me years to understand this—to see it. And so I still say it—Father—Breath—though with a new understanding—a knowledge that comes from release and its stillness—its presence immediate and palpable, like a small dog who follows you everywhere, or a bird, or the seed from a small, unnameable fruit that glistens even when dry—the green refraction of the light within a bottle upended on a piece of rebar that emerges from the column of cement that extends beyond the rooftop of a house in Mexico or Spain.

Father, I say. Protection. Support. Habit of light and object of knowing.

Chapter 11

A Ripening

She is crying. She is sitting on a bench at the park in a sleeveless shirt and no jacket in the beginning of March, which is winter, really, though it appears with a pretense of spring, its thaw and blossoming, its warmth, the steps of the cathedral lit up by the sun.

As I said, she is crying. Her arms are bruised, outside, above the elbows, as from a shaking of hands, and inside too, above the elbows, as from a needle or a spike.

Her nipples are hard, because of the cold, and I notice them.

I do not even have to ask what has happened, what is wrong, except to let her satisfy the need she has in the telling of it. It is one of the oldest stories—yet strangely— as so many things—for the one who lives it—immediate, without precedent or history—something we own and that owns us—our risk and surrender.

Richard strapped the surgical tubing around her arm until the veins grew large and swollen. And then he touched her with it—entered into her, not with his body, but with his hatred of it, his loathing, which is the true shape of the needle and the relief it gives, the life it delivers us from somehow disappearing into the life it delivers us to—and the illusion that distinguishes one from the other.

O how at first she rose with it, her head drooping, the world inside her gone somehow simple, unattached and given, a racing warmth that knew no encumbrance or fear, no warning or regret.

Even in the midst of it she could feel her thighs opening—how she wanted them opened, lifted, as he moved himself into her, gently at first, yet full of disregard, rocking her as though she were a child—then faster and harder—lifting her up with his force and hurry—a hollow thing that took her, that she gave herself to, disappeared in, a pleasure of disappearances, its safety, driving her away from herself, from him, the life she wandered from and into, the secret escape she had searched for.

Now she was alone and crying and he wanted money. Richard was sick. He shook her, he struck her. He sent her out to work.

But this time it was something she did not out of her own emptiness or need, but out of his, who had, for a moment, suggested, by his very gift of vacancy, both company and refuge, which made it even harder for her, to be denied even this, her mouth open, slapped and sent away—

Better to lick your teeth, she said, bitterly, and sat there weeping.

Chapter 12

Death. Just Death.
(The Boat-Swollen River and Green)

His body was a swollen thing, the mouth distended. A shade of paste and linen. Everything about it denied him: the gray suit they dressed him in, the polished shoes and silver cufflinks. This was not my father—not the face or the closed eyelids or the hands, folded, and it was this that terrified me, till I began to believe that if one were to look upon it for too long it might burst or melt, the mouth slip open to reveal the teeth, the gums retracted, yellow, the shadow of the throat like lead or gunpowder, cheeks plumped out with sticky cotton.

Yet even so, the face was impossibly familiar—and this also terrified me: a face of potentials, as if at any moment it might assert its knowledge of scowls and bluntness, a thin smile, a face of flatness and winter, of intersections, like wicker or wool, a face that carried itself or gave itself away, flushed with whiskey and loss. A squint. A lateness. The father's face, implicit, manifest.

A light that flickers before exhausting itself. The darkness left behind in a room a man has just stepped out of.

It is how I know them—these people I speak of here, the desolate and unseeking. It is because of what I became to accompany his dying, to honor it, deny it—a blue raincoat in a black chair—a bit of unpolished tin tacked to the roof. A thing unto itself, dissociate. An emptiness.

This was my vacancy—a memory filled with it—a mirror where women lifted their shirts if you called out to them, the sun descending west of the river, its familiar metaphor. The fresh appendectomy scar above the pubis of a girl who kept moaning, Fuck me, Fuck me, her underwear faintly stained by menstrual blood.

I know how one emptiness can seek another—how it seeks to discover itself—its repetition and reflection like a scene in a movie that is only partly about abandonment—How it seeks itself as a confirmation, of sorts, of its persistence, because it is presence or fullness of spirit alone, their habitation, that can threaten its endlessness.

This was me—

Walking the streets at two in the morning, all whiteness and advertisement, a tourist pouch of dope or money or both but never neither strapped to my calf. One man talking to himself walking in small quick circles beneath the don't walk sign. A young boy throwing punches at a doorway.

That was a long time ago. And like all things that were large enough to fill the body or empty it, it has now grown small, a diminutive yet necessary aspect of the enduring self.

Open your hands, the sages say, so the magnitude of a single event that intrudes upon the mind and its directions, crowding the day, single in its appetite, and consumptive—might become, as it recedes, passing like an egret over the marshes, like a red wasp leisuring back towards the shadows of the neighbor's wood pile—the simple facet of a larger jewel, a moment of light on a body of water.

This, then, is the shape of affection, of grace. A woman in a field of dewberries, palms stained with the blessing that is upon her, what we call fruit, or food, or the light that can be eaten. This is the yellow saucer and the purple cup, two quick birds in the briar. The simple presence of the wind that comes from the north and brings the kind of rain that is followed by the sun—the circle of an instant we are contained by, one mouth greeting the other in the way that mouths have been familiar with for ages: You imagine them: the habit of the mouth. Its giddiness. Its calm. Its familiar cadences. Its dance.

Chapter 13

Bergson and the Gift of a Well-Timed Explosion

I was at the corner market when he hit me. One moment I was holding a tangerine in my hand, testing the weight of its warmth and brilliance, the next moment I was falling, a kind of blackness spreading from my left ear into my cheek and temple, a sharpness that grew almost instantly numb, racing like a cup of spilled water across the surface of a table, disappearing into the edge of things like a twelfth century explorer—the kind of falling that is far enough away for you to know it's there though you cannot hold it or see it and there is something you can sense that is horrifying about this.

When I came to he was kicking me, Wells's hire, and I rolled away from him, crouched there, curled up, to avoid the blows, a waiting deep inside me that felt nothing but a distant form of nausea and a strange sense of the crowd around us, as though a lifetime's worth, the rush of people moving away and the whirring of what sounded like a drill in the air and growing louder.

Bitch, he said, and I could tell he was close to me, beside my face, kneeling, a strange dog whining at his side.

Fire. Blindness.

It was his body, beside me, above, the wall of his flesh, that took it—the heat and light, the bits of metal and fruit, slivers of wood, car keys and purse straps, children's shoes, snippets of hair, pebbles and plexiglass, bottle caps and shit and blood and water.

From the waist down what was left of him was a man, immaculately dressed, his white shoes barely scuffed, his suit pants freshly creased and laundered.

Above the waist was unrecognizable—steam rising from the scorched and lacerated flesh, hairless and almost featureless, face and throat turned upon each other, left hand jumbled and bent against itself, right arm missing.

It is always here—the immediate and its aperture, its configuration of threat or of salvation, an endlessness wherein our mutilations can—by the unfolding of the hours and the days—become our benefit and cause, our comfort and beginning. What appears at first as our undoing, becomes our blessing, or what appears as blessing can become our ruin. Suffering, they say, and pause and breathe, but within it, in its changes, where desperation is motive and vision, the broken moment becomes, almost unknowingly, the impetus of a resurrection—and thus transforms itself and its predecessors, endlessly, one could say, and strange.

And yet—who has not known a man or woman whose suffering has become their friend—become their familiar, in the old sense of the word, an animal that accompanies them everywhere, that watches from a doorway or window, purrs and circles, knows their habits, their lusts, and by that knowledge is their comfort, as though they preferred even this companionship, its abnegations and withdrawals, to their release, to what one might become or be or be called upon to do to live without it.

This is mine, we say. And it is dear to us—reliable and close, and in its constancy there is a kind of happiness, a repose we cling to and love and that consumes us.

Chapter 14

What Night Brings

A dream again. Of thinness and mountains. Of a coldness in the light, a dry, uninhabited slope of earth and stone, a river as green as a pair of eyes, so far below the ridge it is a stillness, an unwavering ribbon of color.

A woman there, in limber slenderness, agility, ties an orange thread around my wrist, then kisses me, her mouth a way of leaving the familiar body, not passage out, but into a new idea of it, a standing welcome, the history of bees within the flower's throat, a grove of bamboo, bright yellow worlds of mustard blooming in terraced squares along the valley bottom. What a kiss can do.

Beauty. Buildings unbroken by the fire. A prominence of light upon the windows. A bowl of cereal.

And in the light, almost indivisible—eros. The

waistband of a woman's pleated skirt conjugating softly on the hips, a swaying of cotton. A thought.

In this sleep, all is confused, yet brilliant. The balanced increment of limbs upon the tree—my lover's eyes, I seem to think, and vaguely, opening after a long sleep, her light blue sleeveless shirt, shoulders soft as sweet cake and afternoon, her illness passing. The sky seemingly clear, but the horizon swallowed by the haze that is connected, somehow, to her fever.

And then the dream of water and heat. Of footsteps receding. Boots worn smooth. A subtle unevenness within the walking.

Meeting 3

This time she came alone. Yet even so, I knew he was there, Richard, nearby, junkie, lover, pimp, smoking a cigarette outside the delicatessen on the corner, drinking a Yoo-Hoo, strung out so tight he had become dangerous, loosened from himself and his fear, a bit of laundry hung out to dry, swaying from the wire, heat bouncing off the black tar roof with the prescience of a mirror, breeze impossible and hot.

She knew I knew this, of course. I could tell. Just as she knew what I thought of him, and what I knew by seeing her—skin on her right forearm like a slip of papery bark, the purple sore at the corner of her mouth clotted with blood-red lipstick.

Are you hungry, I asked, knowing she wasn't. But

it was one of those things you say because you know the person you say it to, who finds it hard to welcome comfort or relief, will understand.

So I was glad when she started to cry, though she withheld herself almost immediately—face returning to its implacable mask—that face that was her habit and her need—the face she learned, who knew how young she must have been when she discovered it, was both her sanctuary and revenge—its fixed form, ritualistic, theatrical and ancient, the mnemonic feature of another world.

It was raining outside, so we looked out the window, silent—the rustle of voices around us, waitresses in black aprons. What a world it was—a young man dressed in a new suit stumbling down the street, his eyelids a bright and lovely blue. A tall man struggling to close a suitcase overstuffed with wool-knit scarves smuggled in from Budapest. Two gay cab drivers inexplicably strolling the sidewalk together, arm in arm. A woman carrying her breast-feeding infant in a lavender sling that criss-crossed her body like one of those insignia that indicate a person's membership in a large and powerful organization. The Red Scarves or The Yellow Turbans. Worshippers and thieves and soldiers. Schoolgirls and government agents. Family members who say they love you. Family members who don't.

Silence. What a woman I knew once loved to talk about. Its permission. Its bus ride toward the mountains.

She defined it as the kind of speech that is filled with implications—indirect, metaphorical—and this was its liberation—the silence arising within the space that has been suggested or invoked by the image and its wording, its inwardness and its outward flow—how it includes the ones you love and trust as a strange, almost unwelcome part of you—a dish of finishing nails in the refrigerator, the water tank upon the roof, the long cold shower.

I thought it was a comfort to her. The turned up corner of a burgundy napkin. The soup spoon trembling with clear broth—the bowl of beets and green beans, bread like butter.

It is my belief that color transforms us—its suddenness and comfort, its near immediacies, how it insists upon itself and welcomes us, its light and shadow, tint and shade, its enduring entreaties. Brightness, it says, is a form of salvation. And so I ordered a feast of it. The green yarn. The gray underside of a falcon's wing. The brown and amber spots in the skin of an apple. Here, it tells us, is always. A golden river of fresh-cut wood. The white and yellow daisy. Sap and blood. The afternoon of the flesh that is filled with them. Goat's milk and the iridescence of feathers. Brief and lovely and our honor. Our cure.

Chapter 15

Giving Is A Way of Having

Mother. This time, mother. The woman and her depth, her impossibilities. The miracle of a woman's body joined to a man's—the transcience that is born of transcience, yet is a repetition—the unchanged, unchanging recurrence we call birth and waking. This gratitude and sadness.

Mother. She who bursts suddenly into flame. Who gathers roots and bottles and old romances. Resentments. The wilderness of the mind in its solitude. The striped curtains, unwashed for years, utterly still within the dark house. The television flickering, gray-blue and predictably, the volume familiar and low.

Sadness. Loss. The voice from the radio. The racing of her fingers through the air, as though she were practicing upon an invisible piccolo—sharp notes like glass and air and wind and nervousness.

Mother. I am here. I have come. Whatever I wanted to ask of you, I give back, I return. You who can owe me nothing—you who were my passage and arrival. With this life all debts are even. Here is your house—it is paid for. Here is your bank account—filled with money and importance. Here is drink and muffled laughter and precious isolation. It has taken me years to find you—to present myself. Here is a candle of beeswax mixed with milk and honey—a candle that burns slowly and smells good, with a small yet pretty light.

Chapter 16

No Ideas But In Things

The anger grew. Quite naturally, offspring of fear, uncertainty, the frustration that accompanies them. People who hadn't smoked in years began again. Sober people drank. Drunks got sober. Children started stealing matches and lighters from their parents, scorching and melting their LEGOs and log cabins in a sad attempt to mirror the world.

I heard that Richard had gotten robbed in a little park by the river. Seems he had gone there, his body the color of tin so old it has become almost collectible, trembling from need and cold, and a couple of guys who recognized him in his weakness, its universal language, forced him down upon a bench and took everything he had—spoon and small plastic vial of water, cotton balls and cutex, a piece of tiger's eye and one green serpentine bird he carried for luck and flight, though this time it was his own luck, and there were other things he carried that made it.

Seems he said something, and the taller of the two simply backhanded him in the mouth with the butt of his knife—one of those the survivalists carry where the handle is heavy steel and hollow and has enough room for a week's worth of rations, a compass, a map, flint and steel, a rocket launcher—and one of Richard's front teeth cracked and broke off, in the shape of a guillotine blade, to be exact, though whether or not this were a portent about his future or a pronouncement about his past, who could know.

I did know it was the same tooth he used to light matches on, the kind that could strike anywhere (like the two men who robbed him), till one evening the head broke off of one and stuck to his tooth, his burning mouth transformed into a crazed grin, lips drawn back like a growling dog to escape the heat, his hands flailing at the flare that brightened there and blistered his mouth for a week.

You must wonder why I speak of him—splashing cologne on his back and chest and throat to convince people he had recently bathed, the consistently huddled posture of his body that was the outward form of his selfishness. The innumerable forms of it—and the hope of rescue, of reclamation, that is its only match. How it walks quickly to escape the wind. Sunbathes in summer.

61

Meeting 4: A Rising

She ate the soup. The bread they brought to her, the basket of it. Pierced the peas with her fork, the beets, because of their color, she said, how the mouth took to it. But the meat she left there. Untouched. A dead thing she was not hungry for, she said, having been raised with cows and pigs and lambs and sheep and birds and the people who slaughtered them.

When I was a girl, she said, we had a trailer—my mother, my sister, me—a trailer that leaked, that shook and rattled in the wind so often my sister and I used to dance to it, my mother sitting there with a big smile on her face, a smile that almost hurt us, clutching her bottle of cough syrup. Family, she would say when the song had ended, and she would open her arms wide and draw us to her.

She told me this—that to touch, meant her mother's hands would close, and one sensed not welcome, but need and hunger, and in them, each or both, a kind of demand, an insistence that would always justify its keeping as a kind of giving.

It made her sick, she said. So that until she was seventeen, everything she ate she ate with a spoon, even oranges and asparagus, milk or chocolate. Energy bars. Gummy bears and bright red strings of licorice. Streaks of color on the plate.

Who are you, she said. There is something soft at the edge of you—like a kind of thread, or a seam, faint with color, a tint of blue, perhaps, like the deep end of the pool at the community center—at the end of the day— just moments after the last swimmer has emerged, and the water—scalloped and bobbing—unfastens itself, returning, slowly, to its morning stillness.

Inequalities of Affection

Richard would clear his throat. Duck and rattle. Like dice in a cup. I can't find myself, he would say, as though the self were something that could be stolen and hidden, misplaced and searched for. A drawer opening. A blanket pulled from the bed. A pair of fingers plunged into a jar of mustard.

Sometimes he woke up convinced there were jewels everywhere. A ruby he had somehow forgotten, from the brownstone by the lake, the diamond he had pried from the collar of a dog. Riches, he said, convinced, almost, that they were waiting, that they were something he already possessed but had—against all reason—forgotten, misplaced somehow, a feeling that tormented him, leaving him perpetually restless and hurried, hunched over the coffee table, spitting into a cup, looking about and licking his fingers on the street, rocking in his seat at the movies.

Somehow he reminded me of a refrigerator, the white door decorated with a red magnet and a green one, a sliver of apple and a sprig of kale, and inside a single Pyrex bowl of radishes cut to resemble roses— and what might have flowered, what might have grown in the earth toward air and light, had been saved and hidden as if to preserve itself, and by that preservation, its fruitfulness and culmination, had been left unmet and unsampled and cold.

Piss on him, he said, as they kicked him. Let me piss on him, he said again, and he straddled the man, the curled-up body beneath him, clutching its violin, holding it as though it were a child, as though it were the most valuable part of himself that could not bear to be beaten.

This is what Richard did, who he became, when he was full of himself, gorged and swollen on the felt largeness that possessed him—turning the things around him into a blankness and blaming them—blaming them because he could—because they were there, and sin- gle, and unaccompanied, and weak, and lonely—leav- ing that old question—is it something we take that deliv- ers us, or is it something that has taken us?

For a week now he has dressed like a pimp from the sixties—like a flower—his hat the color of a lemon, his suit a loose bright purple, his shoes the even green of new grass—believing, he told me, that if he could con- vince the world he was Ike Turner, Tina would appear to sing to him, her song the proof of an undying and famous love that was due him.

Chapter 17

Kuntslerroman #2

Who knows why—but my mother favored the darkness. I found her after three years of looking, the same ruined house my father tracked her to, though different, on the outskirts of Pittsburgh, streets shining like the world after an ice storm, the glazed eyes of a woman who has decided to leave you without sharing a word about it.

Inside, the house seemed to be inhabited by that small sound a fire makes as the coals gradually exhaust themselves, the faint crackling sounds, as of heat shifting, leaving the charred body of the wood that remains there—like the sound of a candy unwrapping, though without its promise.

She could hardly look at me. She could hardly speak. She preferred, it seemed, to weep in her chair, a slender, frosted glass of cribari wine on the table beside her, watching old tapes of Paul Newman films, imagining herself as Patricia Neal, hard drinking, independent, coughing slightly as she looked out towards the sea of grass, bitter and yet tender, a member of that class of people known as the "once famous," a person with history.

I think what she loved most about herself was her sense of failure—that this ennobled her somehow—her breasts slipping in and out of her faded gray bathrobe when she leaned over to light a cigarette or refill her glass or rewind the tape on the VCR, insisting that I pay close attention to the scene she was replaying, saying See, See That. Then leaning back in her chair, satisfied somehow, by what had been revealed, by what had been proven, as though it were this anecdote, this moment, this story that was her vindication, her salvage.

Chapter 18

After Goya

As the girls said—the bruises—her thinness—even though it matched her smallness—the sore on her lip—her dark eyes—the new expression on her face: men looked at her, head and face hovering beside the open window, and turned away, pressed buttons, pedals, sought a different mirror, one that did not reveal themselves so plainly.

Night took on a new habit. For twenty dollars now, she would touch a man with her mouth and keep it there until he came, a plumber with a lung infection, a mason whose hands were cut and bleeding. Now the headlights of the cars made her dizzy. She reeled in them, stumbling from the sidewalk to the street, letting the world take what it wanted from her, taking less and less in return for what she gave—everything accompanied by the faint smell of mold or a ruptured pimple.

One night four men high as yellow jackets and as hungry as lice lured her into the back of their van, straddled her chest and thighs, came in her mouth and ears and on her face and inside her, taking their turns with her, facing her up and flipping her over, holding her waist and shoulders and hair and cheeks till she was flooded with them. A thing she could hardly remember. And yet what frightened her most, she told me later, was how afterwards, she realized the part of herself that desired it, that wanted it again, the forgetfulness of it and its riches, enough money to stay high for a week, she said, attending matinees and twilight shows at the local movie theater, living on anonymity and popcorn and water and pills.

Call

The phone rang and it was her. It seemed she had kept my number.

Let Be Be the Finale of Seem

So. An arm. An exhausted envelope. One swollen eye, but no shadow. You try to figure it out and you just get farther from it.

Her Childhood Too

A girl. She is sitting on the floor of her bedroom, a small plastic oval of round frosted light bulbs surrounding the mirror she gazes into.

Walls the texture of a new leaf—its tint and softness.

Carpet of sheep's wool.

Downstairs—a murmuring. A drunkenness—and a return. A shout. It's three in the morning and the world is populated by distance and the hush of emptiness.

All this broken by a sharp yet vague loudness. A footstep on the stair. An arising.

It's horrible ascent.

Meeting 5: Call Me, the Musical

Help me, she said, her first words, her voice panicked and searching, confined, a multitude of desperations, the voice of a child lost on a train that had stalled on a bridge high above a body of water, a train which would not move again until morning, a great wind trembling.

Help me.

She had come home, she said, flushed with enough cash to keep remorse or sadness or pity small, enough to make the day a plaza of light and festive paper, a table in the sun, confetti of horses and pigs dancing across the flagstone—and found him there—a thin red line of blood streaking his right forearm, his bicep unharnessed, a needle resting carefully on the spoon beside him— mouth open, insensate and drooling, eyes open onto who knows what visions or lack thereof, a man banging on a tank of oxygen with a heavy wrench, a stack of folded papers, the difficult, magnified surface of a green avocado.

It's the way the plastic corner of a bag can stretch before it tears, and then, after it has torn, tries to return to itself.

It's what is left after a person has moved away— white dust in the closet, a roll of paper towels on the counter, a bag of ice in the freezer.

At the hospital they put him in a bed and waited. Took his pulse and gave it back.

Watched his breathing, the mouth flickering, pupils growing inexplicably wide then narrow, a stillness upon him that went unbroken.

Go home, they said, for it is what they always say— for themselves as much as for others—There is nothing we can do, and we know this, nothing but walk back and down and out into the street, its ignorance and busi-ness, to watch the moon darken, the high clouds enter-ing into the angle of its light, the darkness and warning that have become a part of its context and condition, the phenomenal world now pregnant with our knowledge of the thing, poor Richard, his body had become in its stillness.

Crossing To Get There

This night a dream again, of the Himalayas, the mountains steep with light and its journey through the thin air, the fields below us, the plural self with its villages and rain.

Here—with only a pile of stones to mark our passage, to honor the high passes where earth allows our crossing, moving from one country to the next, season of rain to season of drought, tall grass to stone and pebble.

We are like little flags that wave in the wind, our body a colored prayer, a shawl of wool with a word embroidered within it, a word we must unravel ourselves to discover, a new world in the unraveling.

Chapter 19

April Is the Cruelest Month

It's in this bead of agate. This yellow string. A dowel of dark wood turning slowly gray at its edges.

These are the precursors of memory, their shape in the solid world—neutral, unimpeded—

And then—

This is the chair my father sat in, scribbling in his little notebook, gazing out the window beside him at the lizards in the garden, how they would appear, from time to time, perched on the rim of a pot, the leaf of a pea, to gaze back at him, bobbing their slender heads up and down as if in defiance or greeting or both, their throats alternatively swollen in a red display, then thin and sleek, the brightness reaching out for a moment and then returning to the litheness of the flesh, its curiosity, its quickness.

Chapter 20

The Triumph of Achilles

I know you, Wells said to her after she had gotten into the car. I have your smallness inside me, your mouth and your hands, your hips. I have your roundness and what's taut, what holds and clusters, what lets go.

I have you inside me and you have him, and he showed her the scar above his eye, behind his ear, the flesh surged into and over the black thread he had left there to remind him of the knife he would need to cut it.

There was nothing for her to do, nowhere for her to go but to match herself to him, to become his moving shadow, one hand tied to the steering wheel, another against the lowered headrest, as he took her, from the back, violently forcing her face against the glass with that harshness that is the sign of a man's hatred, his hatred the sign of a heart that is empty and cannot rest because there is nothing inside him to rest upon.

Tell him I will give this back, he said when he was

done, cutting off a thin piece of skin from the top of her ear. When I see him. When he sees me.

Who Can Help Us?

The Mayor spoke. He spoke about fire and its schematics, little red circles on the map of the city like measles or small-pox. He spoke about the nation, its breadth and dispensation, its spirit, about women in their loneliness and need, young women, old women, the men who were near them and the men who were not. He spoke about intentions, plans, about history; about madness, like an ant ascending a staircase, about the new world and the old world, and sin and intelligence and the route of mist above the river.

He demonstrated an old technique for cracking walnuts with a hammer.

He employed demonstrative pronouns in original and inventive ways.

He lifted his shoulders, waved from the doorways of airplanes and helicopters.

He searched for things with a certain graceless intensity. For letters joined in a subterranean darkness. Exotic alphabets. The face of a man on a lion. A beautiful woman with a man's genitalia, large and functional.

He wandered the desert in an intolerable heat.

He spoke in tongues, and from the air, through wire and smoke and the tinted windows of armored vehicles, in a special black dialect invented for white people.

He strutted across the grass.

He kissed his daughter, his wife, his chief of staff, his attorney.

Ladies and Gentlemen, he said.

Honorable Citizens, he said.

Party Members, he said.

Hey.

The Hopeless Look of the Sea Out of Which All Miracles Leap

I sat there. Waited. It is what I do when the mind is loose and elsewhere, blind to itself, its flexibility and scope. The sun repeating itself with the clouds' assistance.

These are the numbers, he said—the numbers of Carpenter Wells. His car and license. The tattoo on his back. Telephone and dentist and checking account and wife. Son and mistress. The number of his book and song. The shadows upon him and within, the number of his debt and his payment—of what he owes.

This you can dial. You can press. You can make the light appear, the silhouette, his face, the size of his jacket or his pants, the shape of his wallet, blood type, a part of his memory, a wicker basket of kindling and wood shavings, a match and a camera, a new star:

The movie: Inferno.

The first third, its prelude and entrance, a high-rise burning.

Then the journey down.

I let her sleep.

I washed her face.

I kept a bowl of water near enough to the freezer to keep it cool, ice cubes bobbing slow in gradual circles.

I let her lie there in the darkness, curtain lit up by the sun.

It was my doing, I thought. That he had sought her, punished her, its quid pro quo, its substitution.

Because living is a kind of blindness—where one act, in all its multiplicity, turns back against intentions—a dog with cataracts who sleeps on a pillow by the door, slapping the floor with its tail when you enter or pass by—a sound you dream of.

Good Dog, you say when you bend to pat its head. Good Dog.

And then it bites you.

After that first call her mother said nothing—her concern, perhaps, a brief interlude in which her habit of retreat, of absence, had momentarily reversed itself, the definition changing, the word made guilty and new before its reversion. Her silence did not surprise me.

As to me, I paid myself, and I paid her. When I take the money my father left me for myself, it is an expiation. When I give it away it is a form of praise.

No man knows my anger or my love. It is something I look out of—at the world in its fluctuation and firmness, its faith and superstition—a clove of garlic floating in a cup of water, the roof of the cathedral from my window.

Every shape is a cipher. The historical shape of the dream and the historical shape of waking, the shape of the nightmare that accompanies both—the wooden stake at the center of the village that is the place of a sacred burning, the flower that is branded on the forehead of a slave, the scar in its terrible blossoming. One day the world's truth is a dog or a turtle, a young deer turning back from the highway. Another, it's the viceroy's daughter, bathing in the evening, her beautiful and delicate skin.

This is the stand of bamboo I step from—its height and curl and greenery. This is the flat country, life hurried amidst the tall and flaming grasses. The hill and valley. The old up and down.

Chapter 21

Studying Danger

I watched him. Learned his habits. The bar he stumbled from at lunch, the people he threatened.

There was his wife, Mrs. Wells, expertly manicured, balancing her checkbook. His father and mother, retired and lied to and frail. His son, hosting a Tupperware party at one of the local colleges. His mistress, tall and blonde and predictably large-breasted, a woman he met at the gentleman's club he frequented, leaning back in his chair, loosening his trousers.

Who knew how he made his money—backyard bar-beque deals with the school board and the county commissioner, organizing rallies for the incumbent justice of the peace, trading in ivory and hashish and international currency. A small swimming pool business that paid almost exclusively in cash. A few frightened Salvadoran immigrants. Two tiny Cambodian women in Las Vegas.

The girls knew him. How he came around with his rope and his obesity, the odor of his sweat like a rancid hazelnut or an old scouring pad, drinking martinis from the silver flask he kept in the console pocket of his Ford Escape, holding out bright, pastel colored cigarettes with shiny gold filters, samples of candy for hungry children.

He pays well, they said, and looked at me, waiting. So I gave them two hundred a piece, and they liked it, He dresses you up, sometimes, they said, In masks, the ones that cover your entire head and are thick and hot and hard to breathe in—the rubber slit for your mouth and tongue slick with spittle and sweat and breath.

I have been a Princess, one said, with scars on her wrists, little red marks he made with a felt-tipped pen.

A plague victim, said another, My skin covered with a thick white paste, my arms at my side, my legs together.

I gave him a blowjob once, said a third, Wearing the mask of a bumblebee, and when he came his eyes went blank as though I had stung him.

Sometimes he hurts you, they said. And as though he were hiding from something, he wears the masks himself, a sunflower with a small whip, a friendly ghost with handcuffs, a rat with foul breath and dirty fingers, thrilled by the gradual appearance of a bruise, and paying you to wait for it to come, and I thought—as though it signified, somehow, the inner workings of the spirit, our ability to go beyond our narrow selves, to make some kind of contact—the darkness of the inner life.

Who was talking, I thought, and who was listening. Who was giving, and how, and who would carry it home, the street like midnight, cars like passing comets, their tailings of flame.

Chapter 22

What A Man Gives, He Learns

I must have been twelve, I think, thirteen, the backyard covered with fallen apples, soft and russet-brown, slick when crushed or stepped on.

It must have been summer—must have been because memory is as much or more invention than the day we live in, the mind a lamp of shadow—and because it was terribly hot, and humid, and moving was like swimming, like going under one breath to find another.

From the lilac bush beside the garage the call of a jay, and the voice of my neighbor, Allison, who was fifteen and older and very pretty.

Touch me, she said. Pretend I am candy, or ice cream. That I am melting, and you must get every drop.

Then my body was sharp with it, what is old and has no name, or many—my nose and throat, my mouth, my hands on the soft part of her belly, beneath her shirt, which was also soft, like a thin sweater, her swaying body, the shadow of the leaves upon us, the smell of lilac and the call of the jay, as brisk as a hint of night or autumn or discovery, the sun gilded with its evening phase, an applause of light, ovation, the brightness growing that met us and owned us, its breath both two and one and many, a life of ages, of appearances, immediate and given, graceful, received, taken.

I did not know what my father would do when he found us. For a moment I thought he would call her inside the house, instead of me, the way he looked at her, the way she looked back, holding herself loosely, holding me.

But he said nothing. And when he turned away there was a calm upon him, a rhythm that was seasonal and blue and contented—like the branches of a tree after a hard yet short-lived wind, reassuming their eternal position, the recognition of their place in the air and light, their colorful purpose.

What We Can Do

I dream of fireplaces, chimneys. The cut end of the green branch that bubbles and steams, the song of the sea emerging from the burning.

Yesterday, another largeness, its violent entrance. A van parked with explosives, the city turned by it, tilted, the people stunned and wandering like the risen dead but without the hunger. The faces in their repetitions of grief and shock and disbelief—an exhaustion, and within it, a tenderness—a man with a walnut in his palm and no desire to crush it, fruit that has gone beyond its ripening.

At the hospital then—a new silence—expansive and yet constant—like the approaching smell of rain or smoke—not the silence of the boy we know who keeps his stillness—not the silence of the body and its surrender and delivery—but the silence of the people who have come to claim the dead—the mother who waits in her orange plastic chair, her house keys shining—the three children whose small legs do not reach the floor, their feet swaying, identical, their black sneakers seeking the earth, a place to rest upon.

On the wall, a picture—Gethsemene, Calvary, Golgotha, Bodgaya. Where are they now, goes the old refrain, who built this, who put the little tiles upon the wall, this blue mosaic of delight, these figures with the sun behind them, the first light burnished and clear as a precious metal, the three palms upon the hill in the distance, these beards that want us to believe they are the faces of men with no disguises.

Where is it now, goes the old refrain. The largeness that grew with us—the overwhelming thing that knew both faith and disregard. The silver of a new world on the wrists of virgins, and the history of that encircling, the world of the past and its expression in the current of the air, this current that contains our futures.

Origins

I remember the sea. My mother was there, wherever the sea was, where the sea met the land, where it gave and took, its whiteness and froth, the wet sand in its smoothness.

I moved then, at the edge of it, unbroken, undenied, matching the pulse of the waves and their breaking, daring the water to come and find me, racing from what I called its turbulence, towards what I mistook for its retreat, its swollen face like a mouth opening, its release, uneven and dangerous, shooting forward with a suddenness that hurt and startled, a strained hesitation in the wave before the leaping. And then it found me—what wanted me—this birth that is in water—took me by the hips and tossed me backwards, like a pair of hands that came out of darkness or sleep to steal me from myself and what I knew and wanted, terrifying in its swiftness and force, its intention, absolute and firm and upon me—drawing me into itself—into salt and heave and wave and the mindless hunger that was my source or beginning and wanted me back, always, or so it seemed, leaving me wet and frightened and on the beach, my mother laughing.

This was the sea. The place of birth. The beginning of memory, the origin of my name and how it carried me, and where. This was the first thing. Its ending. What becomes and is becoming—the husk inside the husk that needs be broken. The roundness fallen from the tree. The macadamia.

A Nerve Oe'r Which Do Creep the Else Unfelt Oppressions of This Earth

These are the interludes. The words that struggle to become what they say—pink fork and jar of white oats, boy in a bright orange cap. One cheap bicycle with its bell. Schoolgirls passing in a foreign country. Gelatin capsules filled with dust.

In a place like this—because you walk in circles, clockwise, you might say—there is the sea, to the left, always, at the foot of the mountains. To the right the heights and the slender clouds.

This is your coat of arms. It is what represents you— the part that is larger and is here and has no grammar— no indirection—no object to become or to receive you. Here everything is as it is it is. A roof tile the rains pass over. The braid of color in your eye, and what you see within it, its equal.

Chapter 23

Her Recovery

She stretched herself. Turned over once, then twice. Folded the pillow and drew it to her, a softness that took the shape of her body, her face, a willingness in the thing itself, its kind of love, its closeness.

Soon she would wake. I had watched her now for over thirty hours, her sleep at first as though she had never known anything else, her presence there as insubstantial as mist, tree bark and bougainvilla just barely damp and glistening.

But slowly she took on shape, held weight and gravity, gathered herself, a density with contours and lines and a reviving lightness within her. What was unmoving gradually flexed and rumpled, a hand, a foot, arms that could encircle things, a chest that dilated upon the breath, and held it sometimes, before the long outbreathing.

This place, my place, was a safe place—cameras and codes and alarms at every entrance—stores of water on the first floor—banks of solar panels on the roof—all things wired for space, inside it, out.

We were on the sixth floor—100x30—floors of red oak and white, and granite and slate, everything immaculate, new and gleaming—an openness—a single bed—walls of bookshelves and terminals—a solitary couch in the center—a liquid display that lowered from the ceiling into the room.

I baked bread perpetually as she slept, so she might wake to the smell of it, a smell that returns us, somehow, to a memory of ourselves that is inhabited, I think, by a gentleness that is deep within us, as old as our initial watchfulness, life returned to its openness and welcome.

And I made soup as well—broth both golden and clear—peas and celery and squash the light green color of maple trees in spring—those few days of bright confetti before the first delicate leaves uncurl themselves from the branch.

I wished that these few things would greet her—and that in them—through them—inexplicably—she would find a way from herself—a fundamental and unshattered place of beginnings—companionable, indefinable, yet defiantly hers, an inhabited solitude, a small round clearing that held both blood and fire in a perfect, balanced stillness.

Chapter 24

The Ontology of His Desire

The rope he used was the color of weak coffee or sand, approximately 9 millimeters thick and four feet long, knotted at both ends to prevent its fraying or unraveling, supple and quick and stained, here and there, by blood and cigar ash and sweat and bits of skin.

Sometimes he would use it to tie a girl's hands together—to use the knot upon her thighs or buttocks, or snap it tight in the air between his hands because he liked the sound it made—that snapping that was sharp and sounded painful and strong and had no echo.

It was a language that had overcome him—crude and venomous—and whatever he had hoped to say with it, had begun to speak for him instead—his corruption like a stain at the center of a white tablecloth that is fed slowly, almost unnoticeably, drop by drop, a shadow seeping gradually from fiber to fiber, until the whole tapestry is darkened by it.

I did not know who he might have been once—child

or boy on the stoop in the evening—or how many years it took to become what he was, how many years it took his hunger to purify itself of almost all impediments—but what he had become was dangerous and growing and each day saw new blood—its drawing increasingly without regard—solipsistic—without limit or pity.

One of the girls, Karin, they said, had disappeared. Three nights ago, as I diced squash and kneaded dough, he had come for her, his eyes like dried white flowers, lids like black umbrellas and a steady rain.

Here are your choices, he had said—This mask of a Pharoah's wife and sister, a basket of serpents by her bed—the prone body of a milkmaid kicked by a cow—a countess who must sit in her balcony at the opera, waiting for a song that shall never begin.

He was gone, they said, it was clear, fucked-up on who knew what or how, but he offered her riches, they said, a bestowing of wealth for a few small hours in the arc of his shadow and his want—Riches, they said, and they held themselves, or coughed, searching their purses for cigarettes and lipstick, for small mirrors, anything they could find to keep their hands from finding other work—work of fear or panic or guilt—anything to redirect the mind from what was near and was not wealth, to other things, and to keep it there, far from what they knew had been exchanged though never given.

They found the body yesterday, in a dumpster at the Community College—a blank and swollen thing among the cracked tiles and lunch trays, broken desks and tables and falsified test scores, old erasers clotted with chalk dust and spit and education.

The Art of It

I do not know what happiness is. When I seek it, it eludes me, like the person I thought I was, the person I expect to be tomorrow.

Once I flew in an airplane and was happy. Once I swung out on a long rope high above a river, releasing at the peak of flight to plunge like a flailing, delighted stone into the eddy with its returning waters. Once a girl with freckles cut my hair where there was no mirror, and I could not see myself. I looked out into winter, the room I looked from warm and well-lighted. I saw the sun rise and set in a single morning. She put her hands upon my hips to guide me to her, opened her sweater and her shirt to reveal her breasts there, small and lovely and waiting.

These are the days of happiness. The ones that come, unsought, unannounced, graceful or rough, an inlet of fresh waters meeting the sea, and the life that thrives there—place of intersection and exchange, air and bright coral and transparent waters.

Interlude

Fuck you, she said. Faggot. Freak. Fuck shit. Prick. Look at you. Dick face. Pussy. What do you want, she said. Cock sucker. Fuck pig. Crap.

Don't kid yourself, I said. Whatever I do, I do for me. And I gave her the money again, and my number too, so she could read it and count it, and maybe this would calm her.

In The News

Every day now there were new disturbances. People approached you in the street, making formal inquiries about condiments and jewelry, warning you about the dangers of plastic utensils.

A small group of excitable men and women and boys and girls took over one of the local television stations.

You know us, they said, brandishing their weapons and making proclamations. We are your sons and daughters, historical, familiar. Let us save you from your wealth and misery, from your empty pleasure, your hedonism and your dishonest beauty.

These are the days, they said, When our faces take on a new proportion, the hours of stylish tattoos and accumulation and waste, of expenditure and ennui, hours of savagery and deceit, of large waves and small ones, the sea filled with betrayals and comforts, rooftops covered in thick blue tarps to keep out the rain.

These are the signs. The hammer on the kitchen table. The small spider living behind the calendar. The hair that is not hair yet grows amazingly profuse and swift, the tattoo that encircles the navel.

We are the ones who will take you there—cities and fields and oceans of liberation—past the swordfish inspecting the flower's teeth, the vultures perched on the lights in the parking lot with their wings outspread to greet the morning sun.

Who will join us, they say, And in doing so, love us, for we do not admit any distinction. What the body does is the proof of the spirit's intention—and so we celebrate the body—bread and cheese and wheat and potatoes and roasted tapir—the glory of work—can't you see it—everyone so happy and thoughtless.

Join us. Love us. We are incautious and loud and conjugal. We possess long scarves and curious footwear, satchels and valises and little books with interesting covers. Occidental figurines—characters from epics and folktales, men with ships and girls using matches to darken their eyebrows.

We are peaceful, insecure, friendly. We do not want to hurt anyone. These are our weapons, yes, but they are empty. These are our hands, putting our weapons down. We implore you, let the fire stop. The hoarding. The hurried belly and its groaning. Our sharp yet fragile lusts.

Let us pretend that today is our birthday. Here is your cake, with icing and candles. Blow the candles out. Make a wish. We are born together.

Resolution and Independence

She wanted to see him. So we went to the new wing where they kept all the patients who were sleeping—a large warehouse with rows of narrow beds where no-one turned or snuffled, shifted a foot or a finger.

And there Richard was—among them—and in this way indistinguishable—the rows of multitudes, transcendent in stillness, almost saintly, were their removal willed or chosen. She didn't know what it was, but it frightened her—all those silent bodies, face-up, flat-shouldered, breathing in rhythm, it seemed, from a single machine.

We will find a way to wake him, she said. Anything is better than this. Even sick and toothless and cruel.

It was raining. Seemed like it had been raining for a month, the wooden eaves of the buildings swollen with it, the perpetual beads of water part of the design, one of the forms of beauty that surrounded us.

We stopped at the park on the way home, her large hat covering her hair and forehead and ears, rainbow colored and wool and with a little brim, damp, now, somewhat drooping, darker.

There was a girl working the other end of the

sidewalk. Not a new girl—you could tell by how she worked the street, measured the cars that came and went and matched them with a feigned disinterest, not new, no, but to this place, to our vision of it, and we watched her—the calm of a body that is used to putting itself on display, and knows, holding itself still, available, moving ever so slightly through the air, the monkey bars and hoops and little slides behind it, barrels for trash and bins of paper.

We sat there for a while—watching her. Sat there in silence, a thing we shared, and exchanged, let build and ripen—the room and freedom of it that asked no question, confused no requests. This was our company. The easy fact of it, its mystery, perpetual change, accepted, its implicit acknowledgement, its compliment and pardon.

In a silence like this there is nothing needed, nothing lost or gained. It is an entrance, an offering—an apple or pear or small umbrella—a pause, a place to cross your legs or uncross them, to put your pack down, your purse. Figs and honey—Fried cheese.

The United Nations

Channel 11 was dark. On Channel 13 they were bringing the bodies out, the SWAT Team Captain holding his fingers up in victory.

93

Chapter 25

How I Was Doing (The Road to Santiago)

Sleeping was hard—inhabited, strained. A dream that wouldn't end, persistent, deceptive.

It seemed we left at sundown, and someone tied a green thread around my throat, a small shell to my bootlaces.

The high plains stretched out before us, empty, the dirt road like a pale yellow arrow, dogs in the fields keeping a careful yet threatening distance.

We called her, whoever we were, the woman of hats and whistles—daughter of night and our unknowing. Her miraculous appearance.

For hours we stumbled over stones and ruts and our blindness—the road turning—passing through a field of cairns that rose like slender columns, a city of stones that had been put there to honor the dead, where the bodies, unnamed, throats torn open, emptied of breath and calling, had been dumped like old mattresses, ruined tires. All that darkness. Death. This dream of it.

And then a light in a church tower appeared on the horizon, close to the ground yet bright and lifted. And then our descent—as though from one epoch to another—into a ravine of crumbling houses, roofless, wooden doors wedged open and rotting. Medieval. Short people emerging from the shadows, pouring wine from long spouted carafes onto their foreheads, the rush of liquid parting at the bridge of the nose and flowing into their waiting mouths, lower jaws pushed forward.

They offered us places to sleep. Small dried fish and bread and well-water. Large dark spiders in the corner by the bed. A private bath.

Drink with us, they said, it is free. Get small and happy and old, and never return.

I woke knowing it was late. Or at least I thought I had. Sweat covered me, a slight dampness that lingered in the crotch, on the back of the neck, the forehead and scalp.

I was in a room, trying to leave or enter, I didn't know which—my hands on the polished door knob, holding the light and clarity in the center of my palm, the thin lines tracing its metal outline and habit, conforming to the shape and knowledge of its shining.

I bought a small hotel for them—fifteen rooms as refuge—street-girls sipping their cognac or Chablis—choosing night or morning or neither, old work or new, the street or luxury or both. Food in the kitchen. Bedclothes changed every morning. Cable. Armed guards at the door for their protection.

Your choice, I had said, would say again. Here is sleep and food and a freshness that is free and unnerving and empty—the unobstructed day a day that lasts and questions you.

Stay here, I said. Let the art accuse you. The afternoon. The hour that has no cost except its departure—the hallway and the light in the window.

Do what you will, I said. Here is money, here is fruit. Boredom and pity. Sadness of leisure. A purposelessness that you must greet and question.

This is yours, I said. A gift that is not a gift yet is precious and dangerous, like the openness of the sea and its opinions, a circumnavigation of wind and water.

Go to it, I said. What is yours to find and do or run from. Now.

Do not think I am a good man, generous in my giving. Truth is I wanted each of them, to touch them, in their sadness, their heat, the run of it all in the evening or high noon—that meeting. It was my secret—uncommitted, held close. Laughed at when spoken: large-breasted, taut, dark-skinned, white or golden, brown and slender, wide-hipped, faces sensual and broad and smiling, or sullen and drooping, fat women who might straddle my chest, thin girls who would hold me, crying, after I had called out, perhaps, reminding them of someone they had dreamed of and not forgotten, just the idea of them, that wandering, the quiet, still face that each of us conjures when we are young, with that familiar longing that seeks the eyes and look and mouth of another, that sleeps with it and wakes to it after the light has disappeared from the sky and after it has returned.

Thank God my desire is not the body. That it knows no rule, that it is traveled and worn and knows that no demand can fill it, that only an instant can touch it, partial, before it goes, passing from one form into another.

This is the unacknowledged secret—that it is like light and water—cathartic and lovely and mutable, a motion only another motion can meet and touch, the reach of it moving, always, intractable, yet out of which is born our brightness.

Some people believe that our dreams are the masks of the spirit and its desire—a desire which, if unacknowledged by the body, the waking self, will turn against us and make us weak and sick, as though perpetually dizzy at the edge of a precipice we cannot back away from.

Chapter 26

Messages for the Darkness

I watched him. I'd been watching Wells for nearly a week, now, waiting, leaving signs of my presence—a Xeroxed invitation to a costume ball tucked beneath the windshield wipers of his car, a four-foot length of rope tied to its antenna, a thick, straight line of red lipstick bisecting the driver's side window, and like the horn of a mythical beast, three crushed grapefruit spaced evenly apart upon the hood.

I could see that it was working—how he paused before unlocking the door, or leapt back out of his seat, turning in the parking lot to see who might be there among the acres of cars, the gravel and dirt and cement, office buildings or abandoned apartments.

These are *my* masks, I wanted to tell him. The convict with your PIN number printed on the white cotton strip above the front pocket of his orange coveralls.

Cleaning the median. The waitress with the stalk of celery pinned to the corner of her hat, flirting in Spanish with the owner, who writes her name on your ticket, surrounding it with a little heart, a name you recognize that makes you lust and tremble and glance over your shoulder.

Soon, I wanted to tell him, I will bring you a mask to wear too, a new one, one to cover your mouth and eyes and what you might say to open either.

He was looking for me as well, of course, which was part of the pleasure in it, him, his new bodyguard, the two men he had hired to find me, circling the city in their new Buick, one with blue eyes tattooed on his eyelids so that even when he slept he could see you, the other with Big Daddy branded on the inside of his upper lip, though he was barely five feet tall and drew his strength from a holster.

I had become invisible. The kind of guy who waits for a check to come from a patient and tolerant and wealthy member of the family, then spends it all in an afternoon. Who works the desk at the video palace, the door of the X-rated theater, his sneakers sticky.

It is how I disappear when I need or want to—becoming, at least to many—inconsequential, dressed in expensive loafers with worn soles and a single tassel, pants with rust stains from the laundromat, shirts with a button missing just above the heart or below it.

It is a matter of knowing your audience. Of what they think, and how this directs them, how it blinds them to the real.

Old Blue Eyes

He looked at me. A coincidence. Here at the hardware store, beside the switches and locks and coils of wire. Brooms with synthetic bristles. Corner bead and porch lights and insecticide. Free popcorn.

He looked and then he blinked—his two ways of seeing the world—and dropped his basket—the electric tape and light bulbs and key rings scattering on the floor.

Four eyes, I said, and I stabbed him with the sharp end of a metal file just before he got his gun out—one hard thrust into the heart—then left him there, seated on a storage bin of roofing tacks, blue eyes open.

Big Daddy was near. I knew this. A nautilus shell tattooed on his left ear, the feather of an eagle on his back, spider web and string of pearls, tears on his inner thigh, a dragon on his heart.

The shot I gave him—in the neck—as he sat there in the car reading *Ladies of the Orient*—made him drool. I pressed the file into his palm, the music of the distant sirens still far enough away for me to make sure the prints had taken, his fingers stained, just slightly, by the blood.

Madman Across the Water

When word reached Carpenter Wells he did not panic. It seemed, as some claimed later, he either didn't care, or was glad, going about his day, ordering drinks for the entire staff, rambling to the waitress at one of his favorite clubs.

Imagine a woman, he said, who is like a stack of kindling—her pussy is so dry when you fuck her she bursts into flame—

And then he would laugh and light a cigar, start a little drawing on the bar napkin that people were afraid to see because the rumor had it that if he showed it to you, it was because he had drawn you there—giving you a name and a face—a dreadful looking stick figure with crosses for eyes—a silver tooth or a limp, a haircut, a scar.

Chapter 27

How You Know

What the body does is to assume the shape of the mind. Anything else is irreconcilable.

It is this that condemns me—where taking is saving and giving is having and the shadow falls, always, between them, as has been said, between the intention and the act, our arrogance and our humility, the impulse or the plan and its transcendent good.

The body is thirsty, hungry. The body is full.

See, it says. Disappearance, on the flat roof of a house, at night, or winter, on a frozen driveway, her skirt up, her fur coat beneath us, her husband circling the block in his silver Mustang. This fullness and its negation. Limitless and extracurricular. Love and boredom, meaning and diminishment—whatever we try to keep, to hold to—denies us. Her mouth that was the way down and into, her lips, the elegy of the copper wasp upon a golden flower, a tiny, hard-shelled beetle in her hair, black ant on red brick and going.

Isn't this the object of seasons? Moss and waterfall. A labyrinth of canals beside the abandoned estates. Cunt and Prick. Penis and Vagina. Woman and man and man and man and ageless woman.

She had a name, then, a letter, the breath that began it in my throat and mouth and offered it up, upon her nakedness, her want. I wanted to say it but I could not. This moment and its retreat, its absence. Her parents hiding in a foreign country. Her brothers drunk and without memory.

Where are you? That first tenderness.

This hurry upon the earth. This distance. How we cannot help but leave each other in the end.

Chapter 28

Musical Diminishment in a Major Chord

She was sick. Thin. A rash upon her skin like an embroidery of stars, the filaments of nebulae and galaxies inhabiting the flesh.

It was a new disease—a modern one—or more than modern, less—and we called it Indigo or Boulevard or Nationalization—Oil, Ayatollah, Margin—because we believed it was dangerous, persistent—and the symptoms changed so quickly we were forced to invent names to match the changes as a way of protecting ourselves—as if to name it was to know it, and to know it was to understand it, and to understand it was to rule it. Apple Blossom. Limp. Pipeline. Credit. Global Charity. Administrator.

Such was the nature of it that one day she would suffer a fever and sleep for hours, without even seeming to breathe, another day she would become overwhelmed by a compulsive giddiness and a craving for waffles. Sometimes she was terrified by the glossy finish of the cover of a new hardback. Sometimes she held a paper clip beneath her tongue to calm her nervous stomach. Once she was so driven by desire she sneaked away to the men's room at the diner, exulting in the surprised and grateful look on the old men's faces when she exposed her breasts.

What confounded and frightened us was not just how the symptoms varied from day to day but how they varied from person to person too—making it almost impossible to identify infection and defend ourselves. Some people insisted on spending their weekends arranging flowers they were allergic to, then folding construction paper into perfect squares. Others shaved themselves repeatedly, their legs and hair and arms and groin, complaining of a microscopic infestation, until the skin was raw and translucent, the blood below the surface dark and waiting to brighten.

Obviously, it was impossible to diagnose or treat—to tell the difference between a perfectly normal melancholy and its diseased counterpart, a moment of bliss and a physiological anomaly. Some doctors prescribed rest and hydration and funny movies. Some suggested a nutritional solution that consisted of a diet comprised exclusively of yellow vegetables. Even others—some quite renowned and the authors of numerous best-selling titles—claimed the illness was a fabrication, a neurotic fantasy fueled by a craving for self-importance—or that it was a conspiracy of the drug companies—or the product of immoral living, as revealed by a disregard for savings accounts and the selfish hoarding of mutual funds.

All I knew was she was sick, and I had to find something, someone, who knew how to help her.

So I worried about her—so small to begin with, I didn't see how she could stand more diminishment. God knows our experience disfigures us—makes us rough or beautiful or forgetful or cruel, and hers had been enough to prove to even the most insistent idealist that the world was, at least frequently, abject and hollow.

Yesterday we drove down to the water and she spent twenty minutes throwing snowballs and small rocks at the laughing gulls and terns as they wheeled above the nets of the fishing boats trolling their slow way through the inlet—and she was glad to see one fall—spiraling into the turbulent wake of the boat and disappearing there into that whiteness—breaking out into an almost hysterical laughter at its going.

No Evil Is Wide

Sometimes we live in a world so small there is no room for anything but ourselves. And by this singularity—this contrary and paradoxical immensity in which the expansive self incorporates the world and makes of it a populace of dull, inanimate things, to do with as it chooses—we become a tyranny—a tiny god discovering itself, oblivious to the sheddings of light and speech, the calling out and the silence.

Chapter 29

What Fear Can Do

The girls were frightened. I say girls because it is what they have chosen to call themselves, as if they might perpetuate their youth by affirming it, though I suspect that the significance in a name is not found in the name itself, but in its choosing. Choose it, and it is yours, and that is its meaning.

The police had been acting strangely—nervous and aggressive, patrolling the streets and stopping people they had known for years—shop-owners, newspaper salesmen, prostitutes, drunks, demanding their names, names they suddenly seemed to have forgotten or could no longer trust.

The entire city was trembling. At the edge of itself. Its loneliness, enlarged, became isolation, a frightened withdrawal. People avoided street level, spending sometimes entire days on the upper floors of large department stores, fingering the merchandise with false interest. It was as if the sidewalks had become a kind of running track, people hurrying by in the belief that speed was a value unto itself, as though security and self-protection were rooted in quickness—as in the quick flesh, the body that breathed and moved on.

But it was not just this that frightened them—the girls—the bombings and the changes that had begun to appear in the populace—but something else—not him necessarily, but the word of him. For he had become, somehow, a stranger to them, and they had become possessed by the fear that they would not be able to recognize him when he came, his face, his car or his voice, his hands, even his habits, so convincing had his masks become, so broad and inclusive and unpredictable.

How will we know, they said, and they wept. They ordered beer or gin or plastic vials of methadone. They practiced walking in a stupor, wearing sandals because their feet had become so heavy in their shoes or heels that they could not lift them.

Wells had become a kind of everyman to them— the potential contained in every face, obscured by it, and then revealed, the revelation in its surfacing, the moment of its terrible and empty arrival. Want, we say, because it is an absence, a vacancy. And what he wanted terrified them, because they could not name it and did not know what would remain of them if they could, or after they had.

The clouds moved in. From the north—from out at sea—and what began in light and warmth gradually darkened—blue clouds and clouds the color of ash—a clash of opposites among them, sparks and the kind of cold that accompanies shadow or dark.

We held ourselves—the entire city, as one. We watched the morning go, like a meal we had consumed in a hurry, leaving a mess on the table that sat there—spilled jam and milk and coffee congealed on the linen tablecloth, thick and heavy and stale.

We could hardly look at it. And the silence that accompanied it was not a shared thing. It was the silence of a people who have forgotten how to speak to each other—the silence of bitter lovers and sad couples, silence of disagreement and resignation and exhaustion and defeat—not even worry—what the morning did to us—small and crowded and too close to the earth, this part of the changing day that must be understood to be resisted.

I am a rabbit, someone screamed, overcome by it, and threw themselves beneath the wheels of a passing taxi.

A roar of engines. As though a thousand planes had passed. A tumult of birds. The wet heat of the body, crushed and broken. Then it was if we had suddenly awakened and the world was loud and visible and terrifying to us—and yet we loved it.

Your Neighbor, Mine

Each night now they would tell the children to leave the room, and then they would ask us, flashing a stream of pictures on the screen, the people's faces like grease or wet ice, swollen, scorched black or white, ears and nose and lips like charred scraps of paper or shriveled plastic—their lungs moving slightly beneath the hospital sheet—Do you know this person, they would say. Do you recognize—

And for twenty minutes we would shiver and recoil and watch and pray, when our time came that death would have us, that it would greet us with a kiss and make us welcome.

Father drank. Mother waited. Mother bitched and father drank. Father lied. Mother lied. Mother wept. Father spit. Father drank. Mother worked. Father dressed. Mother bitched. Mother wept. Father rattled. Mother cooked. Mother complained. Father drank. Mother waited. Father lied. Mother lied. Father spit.

What happens, happens. The past, like a beam of light, travels everywhere, denying itself, appearing, always, awake inside us, as much a part of our day as breakfast or weather. Where everything is close, intimate, distance is an illusion, just a kind of thought, a selection. All things accompany us—equivalent, inseparable, evolving. Like a shell or the rings of a tree, we are a dynamic of accretions. The entirety of a person's life— the sum of its billion chemicals, its light and feeling, the bicycle ride to the bay in the dark, the large empty box upon the spring grass, snow in winter, the dirty counter, even the terrible alarm of morning and the carload of laughing girls beside you at the traffic light, the sound that is made when you butter your toast the morning of a funeral—they are here, now, each in its brilliance— distinct, inviolable, yet also qualified by each other, by each ensuing qualification in its turn—a hive of shape and transformation, twilight and midday—the ragged shadow of a potted daisy on the kitchen wall, a chill in the air, one word and many.

Chapter 30

Poor Richard

His father lived a block away, but you could have been his friend for years and never known it. And so his life was a life of flittings and suggestions, a world of margins, inhabited, doorways and dark bars, the distant back of a man in a small boat who bends over the outboard engine to start it, pulling hard at the stiff cord, then turning toward you, for a brief instant, before navigating the dirty canal, moving away from you, making out to sea accompanied by puttering and a blue smoke.

It seemed the indistinct shapes had become—for him—a kind of threat—not their vagueness and indefinable suggestion—like the profile in the glare of the video monitor or the pinball machine, the dull lights of a shuffleboard table with its hush of sawdust—but in their presences—their possibility and appearance—as though his father might, at any moment, step forward from the peripheral haze, might suddenly emerge, appearing before him in his gravity and fullness, a body and a face and a language, a presence with reason and question, with change in his pockets, a frayed cuff, a tuxedo—a response, though not an answer. I think it was this that terrified him most—the arrival that would not allow him to turn away, or to imagine that the turning was not, at least in part, his own. An arrival that would call to him, that would enter into the room, announce itself, speak, bend, step forward and back, make a story that he was a part of, calling it son and father, or fret or want or family or border. Availability. Regret.

What he hated was, I think, the tyranny of it—the telling and the making of stories that include us but are not our own. It did not matter that it was something he did himself—for we believe, falsely, I suggest, that the past, that nation of faces, is our sole possession—ruled by our comment and vision, our bound and circumspection—and that what is ours, is ours, for each of us—it is our truth and what we live by.

And so he is here, in my story, sleeping. Something, I think, for a moment, he is glad to do.

The Fast Life

There were spaces there—a dark blue streak like fired steel, the ground a clash of ruts and gullies and fast ants. Foot stomping ground, somebody called it, a place of hats and strange dances, a place to turn or to stop, or

dangle, a place to let go, to give yourself, away or for,
your hand to the breakfast light, your throat to the coolness of the air, its sharpness, utterly still, the heat so distant, whispered, waiting to claim the day, its waste, its
object—like boots that are made for display and not for
wearing, or a song that is somehow listened to but never
sung.

Chapter 31

The Brutality of Fact and Reason

He cut her hair off. Her long hair, beautiful, black, like a bay at midnight, the buoy lights sparkling, her pale face like a small house with a single light, its beam upon the water, dividing it, making it shine.

Clean the dishes, he said, the knives and forks smeared with butter and cold fat and scraps of potatoes, and he handed it to her, her own hair, held tight, now, by clips and rubber bands, like a horse's tail, though folded, bobbed stiff, yet soft, slick as satin.

The water is hot, he said. Scalding. A mound of suds upon its surface, like ice or clouds, for your hands to pass through, he said, the bubbles clinging to the hairs on her arm, the crease of a finger.

He stood behind her. Put his hands on her hips as she stood there, her hair in her hand.

Dip them slowly, he said, the bowls and cups and plates, till they disappear into the whiteness that hides the water. Move your hand in a circle, a swirl to clean them.

I like the wet of your hair, its thinness, how it grows heavier and darkens, and he put his lips to her neck, the back of it, which was now bare and thin, so thin, he thought, if he turned his head to the side he could get his teeth around it.

She sat there. And the girls surrounded her, gathered round, silent, as she was, breathing, waiting, for nothing really, but what can you say, to see it, a woman's body, her backbone, from the base of the spine to the top of the neck, framed by thin, dark bruises in the shape of a mouth, the tooth marks like parentheses or the vestiges of amphibious life—

It took him an hour to put them there, she said—and five more hours to appear—and she held the money out to show us—two thousand dollars, she said, and two packs of imported smokes.

The mouth. Its photographs. Its records. Like scuff marks. A smudge upon the skin. The shape of a word or a song or a curse. The stack of photographs he gave her, the paper clip that held them like a woman with her legs crossed, lighting a cigarette. Photos of the back and legs and hair. The pretty shoes and purses. Half a lemon with the pulp removed, its soft white edges. A mound of red and yellow pills on a desktop, a little paper flag— the kind they might serve in a margarita on the Fourth of July— propped up in the center, the note on the back telling you to blow on it if you want to watch it flutter.

I am coming, said another, the words written on the picture of a truck, on the door panel, in bright yellow, just below the face that was pressed hard against the glass—one eye close and open and startled—her face, though an expression I had not seen before—just half a face, its rigid, unblinking eye.

They speak of rescue. Of its forms—the shade of a tree—or the old part of town by the river's bottom—the narrow gauge of the valley and the wind that passes along it. The breath. Pneuma. The afternoon like an old tire or a bathtub filled with dirt and strawberries.

Words. Like work and committee and laundromat. Dry-cleaner, manicure, helicopter, church. The earth and its rebellious surface. Its unevenness—the humour of the air and the grass—a young man cleaning the sidewalk with a hose—the language of the water that is made of light and the light that is made of water—those twin vehicles flooding the day.

I am coming, he said, and I could almost hear it. The sound of an old window closing, rattling in its frame. Someone putting a hammer down, carefully, on the back of a toilet. The click of a porcelain clock.

Fine Old Friendships

His bodyguard was large and lived on benzedrine and trite sadist fantasies—burying stray cats up to their necks in the back lawn before he mowed it, slipping an alligator egg into the nest of a swan.

Some said they'd been together since childhood, and were to each other all they'd ever known of love or friendship. All I knew was that he was stupid—the kind of guy who checks to see if the gas can is empty by using a match—which was why no hair ever grew upon his face, which was an emptiness, perpetually slick and smooth, that had no expression even when it moved.

Health Care

The Doctor gave her pills—round pills the color of skin that tasted like malt, faintly sparkling like laundry soap or the lobby of an electronics store hours after closing. Square pills like little pillows for traveling, rectangular pills like storage bins or freight cars, loaded with antiques and exotic furniture, the blue face of a large cat carved into soft wood, barrels of resin, sacks of dried beans.

He gave her pills that would make her sleep or mumble, or stare out the window at the sky and its distances. Pills that would make her sing the tonal sequences of ancient languages, compose startling and lovely and incoherent surrealist poems to accompany the theme songs of television dramas, elliptical pills that somehow inspired in her theosophical rhapsodies and that enabled her to speak for hours into a little microphone her curious treatises about the nature of the soul.

It got so I couldn't tell if she had taken them or not, so closely had the cure come to resemble the disease. It was as though she had become a channel for the ages, from depths I had no dream of, that had risen there, from inside her, genetic depths that cooed and muttered the secret names and origins of things, vowels harsh or soft like a crow or dove.

I gave her train sets and talking boxes to see what she would do with them—bookmarks and marzipan, pictures of chimpanzees inserting long thin twigs into the nest-mounds of large red ants. Twin serpents on a staff of oak.

I gave her blank paper and paper other people had drawn upon. But nothing predictable or measurable accompanied the results. Finally the Doctor confessed, one afternoon, his incompetence, his uncertainty, how he suffered from, or at least suspected he did, a similar condition, and hoped, by treating her, to find a cure for himself, and if not that, at least to find or achieve an illness as inspired as hers, as filled with heat and light, anything that could fill a room, etiological, rare, and was—even if by invisible ears alone—registered, marking the air, the convolutions of the skin.

Twin Dangers

I had to separate them, somehow, the way certain plants can separate the light from the air to become a kind of green and glowing ember.

I had to separate the shadow from its object. The vacancy from the walls that framed it. The face that moved yet never changed from its leash—from the one who had become all mouth and hunger—his throat as endlessly thin as a needle or a pin—his belly horribly swollen and empty.

Chapter 32

The Bodyguard

This way. He stood there, large enough to fill a doorway, to block the sidewalk. When a window opened, or a car passed, he turned toward the sound like a startled cow, ready to run, not away from it, but toward it, as if to attack. It wasn't that he didn't know fear, I think, but that he didn't know flight—and his response to what frightened him was confined to a single reaction—he was like half an animal—a species that had barely survived and was not long for the world.

Still, I didn't want to kill him. And while, in a way, there was no good reason not to, I was grateful for the feeling. As I have said before, I do not like to kill—not the slightest thing—nothing that suckles or flies or races through the grass—nothing that sheds fur or flowers or makes bright fruit. If I find a moth struggling in a cup of water, I lift it out with the corner of a paper towel to put it on some well-lighted brick or tree branch.

Because it is terrible—to kill. I know this. It requires, to survive it, a perpetual yielding—to the weight of it—how it has become something you own—something you have traded for or purchased—and you must look it in the face, meet it—you must welcome it into the house—where you know that forgiveness is not granted or given to serve you, but only another. It is this that is the source of your freedom. This paradox. The contradiction: to sell yourself to the day—like something you once cherished but have relinquished—a book, a silver teapot, an old knife. To know that your life is a channel that is filled with flowing water, and that each day is its vehicle: the leaves and flowers and vines—the women with baskets of laundry—the boys with mud on their faces—the young couple whose bodies are secret and wet beneath their shirts—the hives of bananas, the fervor of color in the air, the passing wasp or egret—each is reflected in the surface of the water—where all things must be given, in equal amounts, the light of your mind, and your love.

It is this that saves me. That gives me to another life, to raise it and to serve it in its stillness, like the first call of a bird just after the wind has stopped.

Look—the skin of a grapefruit—the rough scars like blood—the border where the colors blend and intermingle—the glistening surface of a fired ceramic bowl, the edge of a leaf as it begins its return, the little pictures drawn in the margin of a textbook.

This is the way. My way. My way through you. Our way. Your way. Precious you.

So I shot him in the leg with a tranquilizer dart—watched him waver, let him fall—leaving him something to remember.

Then I loaded him into a wardrobe trunk and shipped him to Venezuela with a tiny camera and a map of the presidential palace tucked neatly next to the gun in his pack.

Exchange Rates: He Makes His Mark

A letter came. Written in beef broth, crayon, eyeliner, blood. Soon, it said, its single word, two napkins folded neatly into the sky blue envelope—one a pronounce-ment—the other, a picture—a single body, hands bound, head down in a tub of plaster, the legs dangling loosely from a strand of rope, little marks on the paper to show how they struggled against the air, a girl kneeling nearby with her mouth open, her collared neck leashed to the arm of a man whose body was not there, but lingered, off to the side, in that indefinable space just beyond our field of vision.

Soon, it said. I read it there. Looked at the picture, the name of the club in gold on the napkin's border.

Time for a party, I thought. A fiesta. A ball, a masque. In one room, a woman in a corset, her small breasts exposed to the light, reading Rabelais, aloud, the floor around her dotted with small tin cans painted a burning red and orange. In another, a man reading Edgar Allan Poe to himself—untitled—a jar of mayonnaise beside him, the handle of a butter knife protruding from its open top.

Come, I would say. Join us—an invitation—a reckoning.

And when he arrived, I would motion for the musicians to play—waving my arm in a flourish of courtesy—and they would pick up their cellos and violins and guitars and improvise, slowly, like dirges, songs called Burning Lamp and Humid and Red Light—songs to welcome him, to make him large and feed his hunger.

The Waking

He lies there, sores on his hips, the back of his arms and shoulders, neither sleeping nor dead.

Put it on his lips, I said, Two drops, and she placed them there, twin beads with the light of the lamp inside them, till they slipped, so gently, as if with an unnoticeable breath, into his mouth.

Wait, I said, and we watched him. Nothing and then nothing and nothing—and nothing more—its cruel permanence—when suddenly his eyes opened—both—in perfect and rapid harmony—and he looked upon us as though he had never slept.

Fuck you, Richard said, as we made our way away from him and toward the hall. Then louder. Fuck You!

What It's Like Here

She was still breathing when Wells poured the hot wax into her throat. But she was dead when he put her into the truck—wet with gasoline—wired with a crude explosive. And when he set it off we were close enough to watch it burn—god help us—till it was all heat and darkness. We knew what he had done. And what he was planning.

Chapter 32

Party Time

Morning. Cold. When parties should begin—on waking—in the dark of winter—the dull light just barely greeted—human figures like shadows amid the bits of steam that rise from the breath and the idling cars.

The dance floor was empty, except for the girls, some ingeniously dressed as their favorite dollar store items—pints of bleach and lemon oil, broom handles, manicure sets, instant soup—some as characters from unremarkable and forgotten films from the fifties—one woman trapped in a sinking car, her face swollen with her final breath, another carried off into the desert by a man driven mad by radiation, his hands and eyes the texture and color of red jasper.

We had disguised ourselves—in kind—as objects—

because we knew it would draw him to us—like the point of a knife left upright in the dish drainer, wooden beads dangling from the twisted thread upon a girl's wrist. We marked our palms with a small red circle, where the lifeline crosses the heart, that we might recognize each other when the killing began.

For me, he was not hard to see, though I could not describe him. Do not ask me why—I have no answer. Not his face or his largeness, or the quiet that somehow raved within him, like the air, I imagined, inside a barrel falling from a cliff—its incoherent frenzy and the threat of its inevitable and violent liberation.

Be Here Now

He watched us, at first, from the shadow of the bar—his hands glistening, as though he had coated them with Vaseline or rancid mayonnaise.

There was no doubt that he knew I knew he had come, and why, both the part that was his threat and rage, and the part that was his hunger. I guessed that he had reached that point—as though there were only two types of people—where he had found all that he could find in the suffering of others, and was ready, now, to discover the pleasure of his own.

His eyes were like the soft edges of damp and rotten wood.

His tongue, moving slightly into the crease of his lips, was like the brown froth boiling at the end of a wet stick in a fire.

When he finally approached me, he bowed, slightly, and I thought he was going to ask me to dance—to offer me a job, a way out, or back, an elegant business card with raised lettering and real gold in the letters of his name.

But when he straightened up—he said nothing. He looked at me. The music played—slowly—without happiness.

I noticed he was trembling slightly—as though some-place beneath his coat and suit jacket he was cold, and there was no heat left to generate within him.

When he stepped to the left, I did too. As when he stepped to the right. It was as if we were joined by something—a similar beginning or end, or position in the cosmos, a parallel will or common dread.

When he put his right hand out, I put out my left. When he stepped forward, I stepped back. We were like participants in an ironic and strangely terrifying chil-dren's game where one is made famous and achieves great individual success by imitating imperfectly the actions of another.

When the music stopped, the girls, expert in the arts of implication and distance and denial, held their hands up in the air, poised like the silhouettes of birds that are born in stillness, or placed them, fingers extended, onto the delicate skin between the shoulder and the breast, the part of the body that draws its power and appeal, like a publicist or secretary, from the things it is close to.

He looked at me. Silent. As though I were the kind of

stain that smoke leaves at the outer edge of a fireplace—
a pattern of streaks and lines—like a blurred product
code—that drifted upwards.

What do you want—Me, I said. Or her, perhaps.
And we encircled him. Or them. And I pointed—at her,
with her short black hair, at the others, scarred, cos-
tumed, indecipherable, holding scissors and hat-pins
and uncapped pens, business cards that were stiff and
blank, spatulas, icepicks, cup hooks, jars of salt.

I will put butter on your face, he hissed, I will set it
aflame, then drove the knife into my shoulder—a thin
knife—for boning beef or chicken or duck—a knife that
was delicate and precise and efficient, a long knife he
started to turn and pull at, as though to strip the flesh,
slipping the tip into the vacancies of cartilage and blood
and muscle, whispering, Dance with Me, Baby, Dance.

I kicked him, drove my boot hard into the bone of
the leg, the soft spot just below the knee. But when I
grabbed him it was almost impossible to hold him back—
as though his wrist and forearm had been frozen and only
now were beginning to thaw, slick and glistening and
cold, and I felt he might use my blood to warm them.

The shape of his mouth was curious—a smile,
almost, before they overwhelmed him—dragged him
down upon his back—meeting him with the kind of
fury that can restrain itself but chooses not to—piercing
him with a precision that might make a constellation of
his body, the shining picks and hooks and pins glistening bright with his dangerous blood, till he lay there,

slumped, whirring like a broken toy, and they slipped the cuffs on his wrists and squatted above him, each, in their turn, lifting their skirts—pinching his nostrils shut with a binder clip—then pissing into his mouth and face until he was almost drowned by it.

A Great Whiteness

I do not know how to say it—but his body had no color. It was as if, lying there, it was able, somehow, to avoid the light, to extricate itself, even fallen, almost unbreathing, from shape or definition or habit.

And then—or yet—it shocked us—she kissed him. His body, drenched in piss, pecked and bloody.

She walked up to him, lying there, and kissed him, softly, on the lips, as though she had loved him once, or still, too, a little.

The sound that came from him was like nothing I had heard before—as if the spirit could speak when it was torn from the body, or like the sound a vacuum makes when it seals itself, if there is such a thing, perhaps something only insects can hear made suddenly available to our human ears—a low and yet ascending murmur that began in the throat and grew loud enough to shatter the balloons that hung from the ceiling above him, the bright red and green and blue latex falling like soggy confetti to the floor.

We looked at him then—until they came—the paramedics with their good intentions, the police. And whatever he had become, they lifted, strapped him to the rolling stretcher, covered him in white cotton, his blood like small red stars upon the sheet, a small glass vial on the floor beside him, something dark and dry and unwanted within it.

I do not know if we wished that he were dead, so struck were we now with his chest and throat and belly collapsed into a shadow—and how plain his face had become, almost serene in its unconscious, breathless calm.

Either way—they lifted him—that mystery that had followed us—that had come after and before and during in its seeking.

They lifted him and took him—and what was left was something we would speak of, maybe, later—though we were glad, now, the girls suddenly breaking down, weeping, making vows, so glad, to see him go.

Administrator

The courts do what they do. You give them the body, the mind, and they are their own confession—the glove box stuffed with photos and napkins, chemical burns on the carpet in the trunk—strands of rope and hair and wax and detergent. Blood, and the name that is in it. That was.

You let them have their own success. The doctors and attorneys and judges. The delirium of a trial.

I have my own understanding—and it is pure, in its way, as though each of us, each day and moment—were both punished and forgiven—for what we are, and what we cannot be—where what we do includes the things we haven't done—or could not—a blend of praise and condemnation that is ours to describe and name, where our burden is to live within its shadow, and to dispel it with the light that gathers within us.

A Revision of the Theme

Birds of the morning. Apples in a paper towel. Water boiled and cooling by the stove. A knot that has no visible origin or end.

It is by singing that one follows the thread—the trench of sunflowers beside the blooming raspberries. Bananas in a dish. All things passing through the light.

Chapter 33

Sky Burials

Let me, she said. And she threw salt over her shoulder—
left a lighted candle on the steps of the cathedral—wrote
her name and mine and ours and theirs on a piece of
linen and then burned it, that we might be recognized in
heaven, the smoke raising us up, our delivery and luck
and blessing.

The sky called to us—the rooftop—its sanctuary
and view, sadness and pleasure and the peace that
knows of either, both. Ashtrays of crystal. Coffee and
tea and pomegranates. Company. Distance and witness
and cheap chairs to sit in.

These are the ten thousand, she said. The slips of
paper that keep us and mark our place and movement—
the basket that is a hat also—the white seam between
the vesicles and sweetness of an orange.

I have a friend, she said. From years ago, in another city now, like me—carrying a soft cloth in her purse to wipe her mouth with, a scarf to cover her face when she cannot bear the light around her.

And that was how she would leave. Like that. To find someone she thought she knew. To discover the name that had been given her, a name that was her entrance and safe passage.

What We Give Is Not Our Own

For some, it is singular, the unnamable thing—a woman in a green sweatshirt with her arms folded, glancing out the hotel window. For others, a procession, plural, a history of automobiles, of color and its meanings, a swarm of gnats upon a rotting plum.

This is the quiet—*her* quiet and its center, shifting, always, like air and light, the arc above her of the sky, the corner table in a restaurant, a chair that fits her body perfectly.

And this is our common, distinctive life—in each a multitude of overlapping deaths, a bird descending, the helix of its single, spiraling wing, his and hers and yours and ours and mine, erratic and blessed, at the heart not vacancy but perpetual fullness, its allowance and potential.

For you, perhaps, it is a room of women's shoes, a Sunday in red, three girls in identical shirts waiting for their turn to dance.

For my father, perhaps, a kind of gain and rest.

For my mother, a flickering light, tin foil, a pastry wrapped in a white napkin, resting on a cup.

In each—call it premise or thesis, participant, dark boots, stone, good view of the water—in each for each and bearing themselves, always on and into and away— a finding.

Today, At Least

A turtle, perched on a rock at the center of a small pond, its thin, dark neck extended into the sun, which is watching.

About the Author

Randall Watson's first book, *Las Delaciones del Sueño*, was published in a bilingual edition by the Universidad Veracruzana in Xalapa, Mexico. His *The Sleep Accusations* received the Blue Lynx Poetry Award. He is also the editor of *The Weight of Addition, An Anthology of Texas Poetry* published by Mutabilis Press. *No Evil Is Wide* is a revised version of *Petals*, submitted under the heteronym Ellis Reece, which received the 2006/07 Quarterly West prize in the novella category, judged by Brett Lott.